THE LOVING FEW

by

Robbie Moffat

PALM TREE PUBLISHING

PALM TREE PUBLISHING
Paisley, Scotland Pa1 1TJ

© Robbie Moffat 2014-2019

First published in paperback JANUARY 2019

Typeset: Verdana 10pt

ISBN-10: 0 907282 75 X
ISBN-13: 9780907282754

PREFACE

Love and romance, action and adventure, the ingredients of good story telling. What the writer fails to tell us, we have to fill in for ourselves.

And so it is with The Loving Few, we take up where the story left us in The Loving and The Loving Child, in a gone-world of yesteryear, when there was war and plague everywhere, and relationships were cut-short by death, illness and madness.

ROBBIE MOFFAT

DEDICATION

This book is dedicated to Pat Trevor.
Rest in peace.

Vino is the drink of Gods and poets,
there is no dispute – men of wealth
sip the grape and swill the berry
while lesser men of fortune go thirsty
or quench their wants with hops and barley.

PART ONE

1

Patrick Trainor was sacked by his Uncle Tom. His uncle had had enough of his swanking about the store in Dublin doing nothing. It was almost as if any little trifle was enough excuse for Patrick to drop everything. Whether it was a visit to the dentist or a twinge in his back, Patrick would show up at the salon late, and always leave early.

Mr. Wylie, the salon manager, would have sacked Patrick in the first week if he had not been the owner's nephew. By some miracle, he managed to hold down the job for nine months before Mr. Wylie went personally to Uncle Tom and said that if Patrick were not removed from the salon, he would resign.

Tom Trainor did not want to lose his manager. He was excellent at his job and was showing good profits after only a year of trading. He envisaged Jack Wylie taking on the overall management of the chain of stores that he had planned for all the major towns in Ireland. It was a glorious time for free enterprise; tax concessions and low wages were ideal for expansion. There were even government incentives to take on derelict buildings and convert them to commercial use, and Tom had it in his mind to convert one old quay side warehouse in Cork, and a derelict mill in the heart of Belfast into shopping arcades.

However, his nephew had become a

problem. Besides his periodic absences from work, Patrick had begun to make a nuisance of himself at the Trainor mansion. One evening Tom had caught him playing cards in the parlour with the servants, and on another, discovered him drunk in the wine cellar. He had initially written off such behaviour as typical of teenage boys, but as time went on, he realised that Patrick was a lazy sod. He made allowances for Patrick's need for ten hours sleep a night, but he put his foot down when he began getting out of bed after nine o'clock in the morning, especially as he was supposed to be at the salon by eight.

Tom, with the words of Jack Wylie in his head, had confronted Patrick about it, thinking that perhaps he did not like working in the salon.

"Naw, I think it great, so it is." Patrick had taken to wearing much of the fashionable items that were on sale. "Look, I'm a walking advert for Trainor Fashion."

He did a twirl for his Uncle who glowered at him.

"Pat, I've decided to move you out of the shop"

"Am I being promoted to head-office?" he asked excitedly. He had visited his uncle's warehouse offices near the docks and fancied himself swaging about with paper files under his arm.

"Not exactly, m'boy. Your going to India."

"India!" Patrick was flabbergasted.

"I've got the three-master *Leinster* taking shirts next week and I want you on it."

"Why me?"

"Experience, son. The *Leinster's* captain's a family friend and he's agreed to take you on as a deck hand. When you get to the other end, it'll give you an idea of the mass market we're selling our cotton shirts into."

Patrick had no answer to that. The idea of India appealed to him, but the thought of having to work his way there was off-putting. "Why can't I go Posh?"

"We don't carry any dead weight in this company, son. If you want a cruise, then you better get your Ma and Da to pay for it."

Patrick considered it for a moment, and then thought the better of it. His mother would not let him go, and his father would give him such a lecture about being a flake, he would live to regret it.

"How many hours a day would I have to work on the ship?"

"Not many" his Uncle Tom lied. "You'll get plenty of reading and dreaming done."

*

Rounding the Cape of Good Hope in a Southern Hemisphere winter gale, Patrick clung to the main mast.

"Trainor!!!" the second mate screamed at him over the howling wind "Get up there you effin' bastard, and get that sheet down before the mast snaps!" He waved a knife in his face, and facing the lesser of the two deaths, he climbed the mast painstakingly until he reached where the sail-line had caught in the rigging. The wind was so fierce it ripped the shirt from his back, and as he leant forward to grab hold of the flapping line, he slipped. He fell headlong. By a miracle, his right foot caught in the rigging, and he hung upside down being swung violently to and fro by the pitch of the sea. Below he could just about make out the second mate screaming at him, when as if by chance, the line he had been trying to reach snapped against his bare chest. He grabbed hold of it, and taking his knife that was dangling from his wrist on a loop, he took it into his palm and hacked through the line. The rope gave a crack, and in a rush the tangled mainsail fell to the deck where it was gathered in by the mate and the rest of the watch. He remained dangling upside down until the sail was stowed, then one of the other hands, Sammy, was sent up the mast to help him down.

Sammy was an old sea-hand from Bristol. "You done well, m'lad" he shouted at him as he helped to free him from the rigging.

"I made a mess of it, Sammy" he confessed as they went below deck.

"I knows what it takes to make a seaman, I does, Pat. They paint ye an idiot, but I don't sees any o'them up the mast in a force eight."

"What have they got against me, Sammy?" From the day they had sail from Kingstown, the crew had made Patrick the butt of their jokes. They'd nicknamed him Pat-Ma-Butt because he always complained to the captain.

"They be honest men, Pat. Not the type to be snooping and sending Jacks up in front of the captain. They know at the end of the voyage their conscience be clear. The captains' old and his head is full of men he's paid off or put ashore. You's young and fresh and stupid right now, like a big puppy dog. But you'll change. You won't be like me yet ... knowin' when's to hide and or when's to get the best out your mates." He winked. "I'll show's you."

"Gus" Sammy shouted across the mess-room to a seaman wringing out his wet clothes "Pat be asking how to make the sail's fast. He be reading about it and can't make head or tail of it."

Gus was third mate, and had been one of the worst ribbers of Patrick.

"Well, you wee eggit, if you're gonna go up ra' mast tae make ra' sail fast in a gale just 'cause ra' second mate tells ye, ye want to be paid mare."

For the first time in three weeks Patrick laughed. The Glaswegian third mate, down to his long johns, his eyes rolling with the ship, crossed the mess and slapped him on the back. "Yer aw' right, pal. God knaws whit wid ha' happened if yid no cut that line."

By a single act of stupidity disguised as bravery, Patrick had become one of the boys. By climbing the mast, he had taken his share of the danger in a difficult situation. Everything was now battened down, and all they had to do was weather the storm.

"But fur God sake, son," Gus added "Ah dinna want ye daein' any mare summersaults in mid-air. Ah thought ma hert wis gonna stowp. Ah've had it wi' Good

Hope. A'm jumping ship in India and shippin' back through the Suez on a steam ship" he joked.

Gus was salty soul who'd had his share of bad weather sailing. He's been shipwrecked twice; the first time in the fog on the Gantocks in the Firth of Clyde when he was a boy; the second as a hand aboard a clipper wrecked in a storm off Madagascar. On that occasion he and the other survivors had spent nine days in an open boat before being picked up by a Royal Navy frigate and put ashore at Durban.

Patrick's ears were filled with endless stories of shipwrecks and castaways throughout the journey, but somehow they seemed to have more potency when told during the height of a gale. The storm they encountered rounding the Cape lasted the whole of the next watch and half way into the next, until the wind dropped, and the sun broke through the black horizon. Patrick went on deck and knew it was great to be alive.

The next two weeks crossing the Indian Ocean to Bombay were the best of Patrick's life. All his worries evaporated after the storm. The rest of the crew accepted him, and for the first time, he was allowed to join in their card games and idle conversation.

The rest of the voyage was plain sailing, and following Sammy's advice, he stayed out of the way of the Captain as best be could, thus avoiding many of the unpleasant duties that had previously been heaped upon him.

*

The ship anchored in Sassoon Dock to unload cargo. Half naked coolies scurried aboard and some of the deck crew was given twelve hours ashore on Bombay Island. Looking to pair off with the local prostitutes, a half-hour later Patrick found himself alone with one in a seedy hotel room near the G. P.O. Her name was Sita.

"You wonderful looking boy. You want to fucky-fucky now?"

Sita had three children to support. She was a young woman with a good complexion. The wing of her nose was pierced and fixed with a stud, and her ankles were decorated with bangles that jingled when she moved her feet. She had almond eyes, peach skin, and straight black hair that fell to her waist. Her husband had brought her to Bombay from the region of Poona, but he had deserted her. She had a makeshift two-roomed mud hut on the fringes of Girganni off the Back Bay where she lived with ten-year-old Nalini, six year old Prem, and four year old Ram.

In less than five minutes Patrick had given way to the slim-hipped woman's charm.

"I no good at it?" she asked him with a pleading face that wanted to please him.

"Jesus, no, I mean, yes ..." replied Patrick. It was his first full sexual encounter but he was not going to admit it. "See, I've been at sea for six weeks." He held up his fingers and counted six, then waved his hand through the air in an up and down motion to signify waves.

"Atcha" she smiled. "You want I get some food for you?" She spoke in that lilting Indian way that employs a side-to-side movement of the head. Before he could answer, she sprang up, wriggled into his shirt (which descended to her knees), and slipped out the door.

Patrick's immediate fear was that she had just robbed him, but he noticed her simple *sari* cloth still draped over the only chair in the room. It was the end of a stifling hot day, and the reddening sky glowed as the sun set into the Indian Ocean. From the vast mass of water came a welcome breeze and the joyous cries of swarms of birds, swooping low over the roofs of Bombay. It was time for the cattle to return from grazing as the doves circled and redoubled and the sparrows struck up a deafening cacophony. Children drove great mud-splattered buffalo across pool-covered paddies, across irrigation canals, and on to the red-dust roads that disappeared into the twilight.

Patrick began to wonder where Sita was when she returned with a tray of rice, keema curry, dahl and fruit. It was all too foreign to him, and although he tried to please her by trying everything, he realised his error when the curry burnt his mouth.

"Jesus Christ! Water! Water!" He coughed and choked and felt as though his insides were on fire.

Sita took a raw onion into her hand "Take ... take."

She forced him to eat the onion, and within seconds he began to feel his mouth and insides cooling. She poured water from a clay jug into a bowl.

"Take *panni* now, please."

"Ta" croaked Patrick gulping down the water.

Sita suddenly began to laugh. "You so funny, Patrick." The smile that crossed her face was that of someone who had once had a happy life but who had forgotten what it was like to laugh. She put her arms round his neck and climbed on to his naked body, made hard by six weeks at sea. She eased herself down on to him and recited parts of the Ramayana in his ear until he came.

*

Patrick had lost track of time. By the time he pulled himself away from Sita it was eight the following morning. He had slept through the gun fired at sunrise, the time he had to be back at the ship. When he got back down to Sassoon Dock, his ship had gone. He stood on the shoreline in disbelief that it had left without him.

Patrick could not appreciate the beauty of the harbour he now found himself wrecked upon. The forest of palm trees that ran the margin of the shore should have caught his attention, the islands of the harbour, their masses of verdure, lost in a soft bright haze beyond which singular hills, rounded and terraced, lifted themselves into a cloudless blue sky, full of intense heat and light of burnished brightness. No, he was staring into the bay at the ships from every clime, fixed in the sunny mist on a molten blue sea, ships at anchor, ships with crowded masts, steamers with smoking funnels, boats without number with large matted sails and covered poops, dipping their oars, carrying passengers and goods in endless activity between anchored ship and the Bombay shore.

"Yes, sahib?" asked the clerk in the harbour master's office.

"The *Leinster* ... when did it sail?"

"Oh" replied the Indian "she went on the last tide, sahib, three hours ago."

"Jesus" swore Patrick.

"I would be very careful about using the Lord's son's name so contemptuously, sahib. He might come down and strike you dead."

Patrick shook his head. He could not believe a native was admonishing him.

"You are Irish, sahib. Am I right or am I right?" He was a small man with a strikingly cheerful caramel-coloured face.

"Aye, what of it?" Patrick could not believe that an Indian could speak such good English, or be so educated.

"I think you should have more respect for God then, sahib. It is very offensive to my Christian ears to hear Jesus' name not spoken with reverence." The Indian looked straight into Patrick's eyes. Patrick tried to stare back, but he had to look away as he felt that the native could read his mind. "My name is Nasir. What is your name, sahib?"

"Patrick ..."

"Brother Patrick." He offered his hand and Patrick was obliged to shake it. "Very good, brother sahib. I am very pleased to make your acquaintance."

"Look" said Patrick with raised voice "I haven't got time for this. I've been marooned."

"No, sahib, not marooned. Bombay is not a desert island. Many think it very beautiful."

"I'm stranded, then!" Patrick was angry with himself for allowing Sita to make him miss his ship.

"It is not the end of life, sahib" Nasir responded cheerfully. "Everything is the wish of God."

"Jesus..." said Patrick again. Suddenly he remembered he was blaspheming again. "Sorry, I'm just upset. I don't know what I'm going to do now the *Leinster* has sailed without me."

"Have faith, sahib." Nasir handed him an envelope with his name on it.

The letter came as a surprise to Patrick. All the while his mind had been churning with how he could get back to Ireland, the Indian had a letter for him. Up until that point, he did not give much for his chances of finding another ship to work his way home. He opened the letter. In it were a sheet of paper and a credit note.

"Well, sahib?"

"It's from my captain. Because I'm the son of a family friend, he says if I can meet up with the ship in Calcutta in ten days, he'll let me work my way home without any wages."

"Oh, that is excellent, sahib."

"I don't think so. Who the hell does he think he is? If a man works he should be paid for what he does."

"May I say something, sahib." Nasir shook his head from side to side. His big brown pupils rolled round and round his eye whites. "I think your captain is very kind. When a man jumps ship, it is very hard to find another ship. See, sahib, no one can trust him. A man, who does not live by his word to return to ship on time, can never be relied on. If all men did not return on time, no ships would sail."

"C'mon, man, I was only late by a couple of hours."

"Does it matter if you put out a bowl to catch water for drinking when the rainstorm is over and the sun is shining? Would a man not go thirsty? No, sahib, you have missed the boat. You have money to go to Calcutta?"

"I've been left one of my uncle's company credit notes. Five hundred rupees."

"Oh, that is more than enough, sahib" he exclaimed in a pleased tone. "You could see all of India for that." Nasir was delighted that Patrick was about to take his advice and go to Calcutta. "Four days by train to Calcutta. One day more in Bombay. Two days Calcutta? Oh goodness me, you have three days extra. Why not see the Taj Mahal, the most beautiful building in all India? And the Himalayas and tea-plantations in Darjeeling?"

By the time Patrick was ready to leave the harbour-master office, Nasir had planned his whole itinerary. He had sketched it out in great detail for him on the back of a map of India, even down to the times of the trains. He took pains to warn Patrick that the trains did not always run on time and that quite calamitous things happened frequently, but that besides *dacoits* robbing and murdering passengers, floods washing away the tracks, and passengers falling off the roof to their deaths, it was the railway that was revolutionising India.

"Yes, sahib, twenty two bridges, twenty five tunnels, just to get out of Bombay!"

"You sound as though you should be working with the trains."

"The pay, sahib, it is diabolical. It is better to have dedicated boys running the railroads and well-paid men keeping the shipping lanes open." Nasir grinned.

As Patrick cashed in his credit note at Grindlay's Bank, he felt positively fortuitous. Being the nephew of a textile tycoon had its advantages. The captain had not dared to abandon him in India without money or a way home.

At first glance there was nothing peculiar in the appearance of the streets. Neat broughams and carriages so common at home were everywhere. The natives rode around in such vehicles drawn by the best horses, with the servants standing upright behind. Wooden *garies* with Venetian blinds, buggies, buffalo carts and wagons, and quaint little native conveyances crammed full, ran up and down the dusty streets. Crowds of loin-clothed coolies, their legs like cranes; white-robed, soft-skinned, wide-eyed Parsees with white stockings and polished shoes; bare-footed, bare-chested Hindus, fine-looking, turbaned, and holding white umbrellas, waddling along with their toes turned out; this was Europeanised Bombay where no-one bore arms, wore splendid dresses, but where every nook and cranny was stacked with bales of cotton. The stores were full of goods from the looms of England with scarcely anything more fashionable than calico. From what Patrick saw, his Uncle's shirts would have no rival in Bombay.

Restless after the weeks on ship, he walked in the warm water along the palmed beach of Back Bay, his boots tied round his neck. He passed along Millionaire Row, land reclaimed from the sea on which huge Swiss like cottages had been built to house the rich. Enormous sums of money had changed hands for the rent of these houses, making it one of the most expensive places in the world to live.

Attracted by three towers on a hill at the end of the bay, Patrick climbed the slopes of Malibar Hill passing by bungalows occupying considerable space of ground, generally concealed from one another by trees. He rarely saw a soul in the vicinity of the houses, the odd servant or group of native children playing in the sun. At last he came to the Towers of Silence, three in number, massed like the ancient fighting peel towers of Ireland. They were situated among scattered palm trees.

Each stood about forty or fifty feet high, and as many feet across. Patrick peered up to see a grating like shelf carrying round the summit of one of the towers, which sloped inward towards the centre, opening to the ground below. To his sudden horror, on the shelf he saw dead bodies laid in a certain order according to age and sex. They lay exposed to the sky, and there was a putrid smell of decay. However, most of the bodies had not rotted away, they had been devoured by vultures.

Patrick was greedily watched by flocks of vultures sitting in the crowns of palms. One or two floated lazily in the sky above. Patrick reeled back in disgust, but as he did so, two priests arrived carrying the body of a child, and without glancing at him, ascended the stairs to the top of one of the towers. The flocks of vultures clustered as thick as bats among the leafy tops of the nearest palms until the priests descended from the tower. Then the air became dark with their wings as they swooped to feast.

It was not mere prejudice that filled Patrick with disgust as he left that horrible spot. It grossed his senses to discover that the Parsees chose to have their loved ones torn by vultures rather than have them concealed in the earth. It was not a matter of worms or vultures. It was the public display of the horrific, the lack of sympathy, the absence of ceremony when coping with death. There was to be no fond memory of a last resting place. In Ireland he could visualise a grave for his mother or father beside the rest of the kin, in the silence of a Kerry glen, ferns drooping their graceful forms, a turf of heather blooming near the headstone, while young lambs played nearby, and a curlew hung high over the grassy mound in cheerful song. But in India, life appeared to have no value, and in death, no meaning.

Returning to the city, he passed through the native town where he thought that Sita must live. No Connemara village of the worse kind could equal the poverty he saw. The huts, barely four foot tall, covered with palm leaves. The naked children with their naked fathers and miserable looking mothers, together with the absence of all attempt to give a decent look to their huts. They hid when Patrick walked past. The women pulled the veil of their saris in over their faces. Children playing ancient games with pebbles scurried away like rats. Vermin, centipedes, cockroaches, flies; every type of insect and creature stalked the slum town for a meal, sometimes providing a meal for other bugs or vermin. Many of the hovels were barely one yard wide and two yards long. The floors were of beaten earth, and through the gaps in the roofs, shafts of sunlight penetrated the furniture-less interiors of the windowless huts. Yet on nearly every doorstep, were the signs of some type of industry, cleaning, mending, making, sorting, and tinkering. There was no running water, only a small shallow groove from each hut running into a stagnating open drain full of brown slime. Here and there was a goat or chicken feeding on thin sprouting weeds or grass seed. Everything else was eaten by the gangs of pigs that roamed freely between the huts eating faeces and human waste, ugly looking black-haired creatures covered in filth and attended by a horde of insects. But for a little daily rice and the daily presence of the sun, the shantytown lived precariously on the edges of Hell.

He returned to the hotel near the G.P.O. where he had spent his time with Sita. Someone went to tell her that he had returned. An hour later she appeared, and they carried on where they had left off, talking about their lives, having sex, lying about this or that, so as not to hurt or offend each other during the short time he had left in Bombay.

Patrick wanted to know more about her life, but he was frightened to ask. What he had seen that day was the only life that Sita knew, and he did not want to discover that mongst the poverty, lived human beings with the same aspirations and hopes as her. He had to look after himself, and turn a blind eye to the suffering of the world. So he took her in his arms, and in a moment of clear-sightedness about the shortness of life, he recited softly into her ear the second verse of Tennyson's *The Charge of the Light Brigade*.

> Theirs not to make reply,
> Theirs not to reason why,
> Theirs but to do and die,
> Into the Valley of death
> Rode the six hundred.

Whether she understood or not, Patrick did not know. When dawn came up she said she had to return to her children and slipped into her sari. He gave her twenty rupees, but she would not accept it, saying that it was too much. He gave her the money just the same, and watched from the hotel balcony as Sita passed down the narrow street homeward towards the Back Bay slum.

2

The brand new Victoria Railway Terminus, Bombay, was much too magnificent for a seething crowd of railway passengers. Patrick felt dwarfed by it. In all his life he had never seen such a grandiose building. It was the epitome of British influence in India, a monstrous red sandstone fortress, three stories high, blending Venetian, Gothic and Indo-Islamic styles all in one, with columns of Rubislaw granite from Aberdeen designed to give the whole giant pavilion a touch of sternness.

Patrick didn't have time to look at anything as he was jostled and pulled this way and that by porters viewing to carry his small knapsack containing a razor, a comb, a towel, and a change of shirt.

"Piss off" he shouted at them angrily. He had been kept awake all night by Sita and the heat of the midday sun was making him irritable. Bombay was getting to him. Like everyone else who had ever visited India, the poverty appalled him. It made him choke.

Suddenly, he noticed that a small crowd had gathered just to the side of the main entrance to the station. A group of jugglers had set themselves up for a performance. One fellow beat the tom-tom with his fingers, in that strong fingered telling form that evicts a sharp and loud ring. Another played a doleful tune on a flageolet, while a third squatted over a set of baskets.

True to every country, and to all classes, whether honest man or cheat, all are attracted by men with sleight of hand and the ability to deceive. They do not pretend that they are anything else than deceivers, and such men are full of interest to everyone. They gather a crowd with ease, and Patrick, despite belonging to a different world, like everyone else pushed forward with the hope of unravelling their charades.

A cobra pushed its head up out of one of the baskets, while a large six foot long rock snake coiled its length around the charmer with the baskets. He had a face that concealed a pot-pouri of characters, possibly good, but most certainly also bad. Even to the crowd of Indians watching intently, these men were a band of gypsies, who in common with their kind in the West, had been outside the circle of common Indian life for centuries.

With the tom-tom beating and the pipe playing, the loin-clothed charmer, with the snake still wrapped firmly round him, smoothed a place out in the gravel before him. Having thus prepared a bed for a plant to grow, he took a basket and placed it over the prepared place, and covered it with a thin blanket. All the while he sang, and just as he became more earnest in his song, he rose and stepped forward and beckoned Patrick to examine the basket. Entering into the spirit of the moment, Patrick examined the basket of open wicket work. He then studied the cloth covering. It was thin, almost transparent, and Patrick found nothing concealed in it.

Patrick handed the basket and cloth back to the charmer, fixing his gaze so intently on the cloth, that he was sure the trick could not possibly succeed. The charmer placed the basket on the prepared spot, then squatted down, stretched his naked arms under the basket, singing and smiling as he did so, and when he lifted the basket off the ground, behold, there was a green plant about one foot high.

Satisfied with the applause, the charmer went on with his singing. Having given his plant time to grow, he again lifted the basket, and the plant was miraculously two feet high.

"Wait a little longer, sahib" he shouted to Patrick "and you can taste the fruit!"

Almost as if the crowd had seen it a dozen times and still could not work out how it was done, they told Patrick that the result would be obtained, and Patrick laughed and said

"It beats me how you did that, for sure. I believe you."

Patrick examined the ground and found it smooth and unturned. Apparently delighted with his surprise, the juggler stood up laughing. The pipe player chucked a pebble at him, which he put into his mouth. The pipe player rose, and walking backwards, produced from the charmer's mouth a cord of silk twenty yards or so in length. With his hands behind his back, he further produced from his mouth two decanter stoppers, two shells, a spinning top, a stone, followed by a long jet of fire!

A mere Kerry boy, Patrick was astonished. He threw five rupees onto their collection cloth.

How, thought Patrick, could he ever explain to anyone who had never been there, what India was like? After two days he felt as though he had been there all of his life. The country was a seething mass of humanity, poor, hungry, and worst of all, ambitious. Everyone appeared to want to do better for themselves, escape their poverty, and if it meant stepping on some equally poor unfortunate, then it was God's will. Which God this was Patrick was not sure, for he was not interested in their religions, and as such did not understand that all the Gods in India were one God.

Inside the airy domed edifice of the terminal building, he was relieved to encounter some fellow Europeans. It was a party of two gentlemen and a lady with a mountain of cabin-trunk luggage heatedly discussing terms with some coolies.

"Excuse me" Patrick interrupted them "Are you going to Delhi?"

The lady turned and appeared relieved at seeing another European face. Like Patrick, she was young, a little older, perhaps about eighteen or nineteen. One of her companions also turned to look at him.

"Heavens, man, can you help to sort this mess out" He threw his hands up in the air. The heat had got to him and he looked very pale and sickly. He was about double the age of the girl, and from the resemblance, they looked like father and daughter.

The third member of the party had his back turned to Patrick and was extremely agitated. He was showering a torrent of abuse on four very thin natives who had obviously carried their luggage into the terminal.

"You swine! You filth! Take that! And that!"

He began beating the natives with his cane as if they were dogs. The noise of the cane as it came down on the unfortunate coolies echoed in the vast chamber.

The coolies immediate began a hullabaloo, part from the pain of the beating, but most from the fear of further abuse. They scattered like terrified animals, falling over themselves to avoid the blows being metered on them by the European. They regrouped at a distance and cursed him in Gujarat and the language of the Western Gnats and would most certainly have continued to do so if they had not caught sight of the arrival of the khaki-shorted railway police. They fled without payment, hotly pursued by the red-turbaned native law enforcers.

"There!" declared the man with the cane to his appalled companions "That's how to deal with the wogs!"

Patrick could not believe his eyes. It was Diarmid Wellesley!

It took Wellesley some moments to recognise Patrick Trainor. Patrick saw it in his eyes. They froze, and then almost instantly they narrowed as he tried to work out why he was in India. He let out an involuntary sneer.

"That was absolutely unnecessary, Diarmid"

said the girl angrily."

"Oh, be quiet, Maud. Diarmid knows what he's doing. He got us here safely, didn't he?" Her father was in obvious awe of Wellesley.

Wellesley's sneer turned into a conceited smile. Patrick hated him, hated him so much that he felt like grabbing him by the throat and squeezing the life out of him. But he was a big man. He had been captain of the school cricket and rugby teams, and no one had ever dared to challenge his authority because of his foul temper. If he disliked something, he lashed out at it.

"What have we here" he snapped pushing the tip of his cane against Patrick's chest. "A Paddy, if I am not mistaken."

Patrick stood his ground. His first reaction was to grab the cane from his grip and break it in two. His second reaction was to reach for the knife he had sheathed in his belt. No, he thought, he had a much better plan. He would play along with Wellesley, and when the moment came, he would humiliate him in front of his friends.

"Irish, and proud of it" stated Patrick.

Wellesley lowered his cane. He had managed to convince himself he was English. He had got it into his head that he could not progress socially if got about that he was Irish. There was a stigma attached to being Irish, people wondered about Irishmen's loyalty to the Empire. It was not enough for him to be British; he had to be more English than the English if he was to rise to the highest echelons.

"So are we ... we're from Mayo" declared

the sickly man "John Diver ... and this is my wife Maud."

Patrick gave his name and they shook hands. Wellesley declined to offer his hand.

"Sahibs! Mensahib! The train for Delhi has come!" An old wallah came running towards them. He snapped his fingers and a group of coolies sprang forward to carry the luggage towards the train. "Come, Sahibs and Mensahib, I have reserved a carriage for you."

Patrick, encouraged by the Divers, joined the entourage as it fought its way past the second, third and fourth-class carriages to reach the first at the head of the train. They were guided into a compartment the old wallah had placed two coolies inside to guard.

"Very good seats, Sahib. Smoke from engine not too black in this compartment. You want chai, sweets, curd?"

The old man had a glorious white beard and a head capped by a white linen turban. His blue eyes sparkled like diamonds. "My father was a British man" he chatted as one of the coolies was sent to fetch some water for John Diver who was looking more ill than before. "You not look so good, Sahib. Maybe, you stay in Bombay. It is very hot now, and Delhi two days away."

John Diver's mind was made up; he was going to Delhi, then on to Simla in the hills. It would be out of the heat of the plain, and besides, his wife's aunt Lady Dufferin, was the Vicereine.

Immediately on hearing this, the old man fell to the floor of the carriage and touched the feet of Maud Diver. Wellesley went to hit him with his cane, but Patrick put his arm up to block the blow.

"No understand, sahib" said the old man on bended knees "I honour the family of Viceroy."

"Get up, you smelly bag of rags" Wellesley snarled.

"If you say so, sahib. Thank you." He bowed and continued to bow, all the time edging backwards out of the carriage on to the platform. Once firmly placed on the platform, he signalled Patrick to lean out of the window.

"He very bad man, that sahib" he whispered indicating Wellesley. "Maybe he not find the rest of India so forgiving of his temper."

Patrick nodded in agreement. The old man shook his head back and forth. Then the water arrived in a clay pitcher. The old man tried to pass it to John Diver, Wellesley knocked it from his hand, and it smashed on the platform.

"You don't know where that water's come from!" he warned Diver. "It might make you worse."

Patrick looked at John Diver and thought that nothing could possibly make him worse. He looked dehydrated. The old man ordered the coolie to get more water.

"He must drink, sahib" said the old man to Patrick. "The water comes from the railway restaurant kitchen. It is very clean."

Second time around, John Diver gladly took the water. He revived slightly.

"Train is leaving now, sahibs" The old man

spoke directly to Wellesley.

Wellesley ignored him, pretended that he was not even there.

"Aren't you going to pay him, Diarmid?" asked Maud.

"I only ask for five rupees, sahib."

"He can go to hell!" he snarled.

"That is not very nice thing to say, sahib. Three rupees."

The train had begun to move, and the old man ran alongside with his hand held out.

"Two rupees, sahib" he pleaded.

Wellesley looked the other way. "Damned insolent natives!" he hissed.

The train gathered speed, and the old man continued to trot along the platform asking for payment. Patrick reached into his pocket, withdrew a ten rupee note and thrust it into the old man's hand. The old man shouted with glee, and in a thank-you gesture, clasped his two hands together and shouted "Nameste, sahib. God save the Queen!"

Patrick hung out the carriage window until a bend in the line took the old man from view. The train trundled through an endless series of tunnels as it climbed the two thousand odd feet of the Ghats. Wellesley sat glaring at him, and Patrick, knowing that a showdown with him was inevitable, engaged Maud Diver in conversation until they were over the Ghats and the heat of the afternoon made talk unbearable.

*

John Diver lay on an upper bunk in the carriage for nearly the entire journey, with a sickness that made him vomit. As the hours went by his condition deteriorated.

Patrick had thought to descend from the train at Agra, and from there travel the short distance to the Taj Mahal, but the plight of John Diver, and the wolf's eyes Wellesley had for his wife, made him stay on the train all the way to Delhi.

Wellesley was far from pleased. He had taken up with the Divers at Suez. He had briefly met them at Giza while doing a tour of the Pyramids, and befriended them when he discovered they were taking the same Bombay-bound steamer. Diver had taken to him immediate, but Wellesley's real interest in the couple had been Mrs. Diver. They had got on well, and Wellesley fancied that if Diver were out of the way, he could have his way with her. It was therefore with some pleasure that he relished the prospect of Diver being fatally ill; for Maud Diver appeared to be a very vulnerable creature, open to suggestion and manipulation.

The sudden appearance of Trainor had upset his plans. Besides the animosity that existed between them over the trial in Ireland, Wellesley had become increasing jealous of Trainor as he monopolised Maud's time on the train. When he finally managed to gain her attention, it always seemed to be with something crass and tactless.

"Some of these Maharajah's are unbelievably fat. I heard that one of them was so fat, that when he wanted to marry, there was worry that he would not be able to consummate the marriage. Do you want to know what they did" Wellesley's mouth watered. Seedy descriptions of sexual inabilities enhanced his feeling of sexual superiority. "To save the dynasty they studied the elephants. Elephants! " he cried. "I ask you. Would you want to be compared with an elephant."

"And?" asked Maud Diver. It appeared that she had a strong interest in sexual matters, perhaps because of her husband's indifference to it.

"Female elephants find a slope to lean against so the old boy doesn't have to slog at it so much. The local engineer, an Englishman I might add, made the Maharaja a reclining bed of wood and steel. He did a rehearsal with one of his courtesans, and it worked so beautifully, he married her, and out popped an heir nine months later."

"Goodness." Maud wanted to hear more. "Then what happened?"

"She was given a pension for life and the Maharaja, flushed with success, amassed a *zenana* of three hundred wives."

Maud was agog at the thought of it. "How awful. Would you like to take care of as many wives as that, Diarmid?" she asked with a bat of her eyelids.

"Only after it got dark."

Patrick sensed that there was already something between Maud Diver and Wellesley. However, she just seemed to be an innocent flit, not meaning much by it, bored by her husband's disinterest in sex, frustrated by her own needs to have it.

Patrick, like Wellesley, was also attracted to

her. She had chocolate box prettiness, reddish-blonde curls, and big blue eyes, and large rubber lips made for kissing. She had a small gap between her teeth that reminded Patrick so much of the girls back home. When she hiked up her skirt to take a look at John from time to time, he could see she had beautiful legs.

"Why are you in India, Pat?" she asked him

Patrick did not want to be embarrassed by saying he had been with a prostitute and his ship had sailed without him. Wellesley would sneer at him. He had to be more inventive.

"My Uncle Tom imports and exports from India. He takes cotton, muslins, and chintzes to Ireland, makes them into shirts and dresses and ships them back to India to be sold." This was more or less the truth. "He's sent me out to see if I can expand the business."

"You look as though you're destitute." Wellesley was calling his bluff.

"I was told you should travel light in this heat. Look at the trouble your baggage caused you back at the station. What are you in India for, Wellesley?"

Wellesley ignored the question.

"John and I are here for a couple of years" Maud disclosed, "He's been given a government post. We had to bring all those things with us."

"Jesus, it must be a big post" he joked.

"Shut up, Trainor" Wellesley told him. "Can't you see your upsetting her."

She looked at Patrick and smiled with puckered lips that made her look quite vulnerable. She was obviously concerned about her husband, and Patrick could see that she was worried he might die.

By the time they arrived in Delhi, John Diver had to be carried off by some porters. Patrick, seeing the difficulty of their plight, offered to help the Diver's to get to Simla. It was only a half-day's journey away, and Patrick argued, with few European's left in Delhi, her husband would have a quicker recovery in the cooler air of the mountains. Wellesley pulled him aside.

"What are you playing at, Trainor."

"What's the matter with you, Wellesley? Decided you're too good for peasant girls?"

"Get out of my life, you little bastard!" Wellesley hit him across the face with his cane, which flung him against a carriage. Maud Diver saw the whole thing. Patrick reacted quickly.

"Come, Mrs. Diver" he said taking her by the arm "we must find out how we can get you and Mr. Diver to Simla as quickly as possible."

"Oh, Pat, thank goodness you know what to do." She gave Wellesley a glaring glance that showed she was disappointed in his behaviour.

It was fortunate that they had arrived in time to catch the morning train for Ambala, at the foot of the Simla hills. John Diver was carried to it followed by Maud and Patrick. Wellesley disappeared into the crowd.

"What a strange man" said Maud about Wellesley? "He never even said goodbye."

The train began for Simla. It was crowded

with Europeans, and they had made room for the sick man and his wife in first class. There was a large contingency of army officers and civil servants making for the hills.

"Is it always this busy?" Patrick asked a derby-hatter Anglo-Indian civil-servant.

"It's Saturday. I'm going up to see the wife and kids." He flicked open his copy of the Morning Post and began to read.

"It reminds me of London at the week-end, except for the heat and lack of fog" whispered Maud quietly. Patrick could not take his eyes off her lips. There was something so exquisitely beautiful about her big rubber lips, the way they twitched and seemed to have a life of their own independently of Maud Diver. "I've been so bombarded with conflicting information about shoes and slippers. I was told it was impossible to get nice ones in India, and I was told if I didn't bring my own, I wouldn't be able to go on hunting expeditions and the like. So to be on the safe side, I brought forty-seven assorted pairs of footwear."

They both laughed. Patrick could detect a slight hint of an Irish accent, but to all purposes, Maud Diver spoke a sweet kind of English. "My huge cabin-trucks are crammed with garments suitable for every possible contingency of climate and circumstance. I'm willing to enjoy a little discomfort for the sake of experience. I'm not going to be a lolling, vapid, washed-out, poor useless creature, like most of the women in the old Anglo-India days."

Patrick felt cheered by Maud's spunk, even though it did sound like boarding-school indoctrination. He had no fears that she would survive the rigours of India. She was too imbued with the Anglo-Irish feeling of independence, too fond and spirited of healthy excitement to permit herself to subside into the slothful habits of the poor native harem ladies or the lackadaisical memsahibs of yesteryear.

"It's John I worry about. We married six months ago and this is supposed to be our honeymoon. Already he's lost interest in me. If he dies, then I suppose I will return to England to find another husband, for from what I hear, India is not the place to come anymore to find a decent man."

A sense of fatalism had swept over Maud Diver. India had begun working on her to the extent that she was willing to accept things as she found them without enthusiasm, and without criticism. If her husband died, then that was the way of the world.

"Cheer up, Maud" Patrick told her, but as the train trundled along, he found it difficult to remain cheerful himself. The same feeling of *que sera sera* was creeping up on him too. The heat was oppressive, but late in the afternoon as they transferred to a charábanc for the last leg of the journey up into the mountains, it rained, and from there on in it got progressively cooler as they travelled over the Siwalik's and beyond into the foothills of the Himalayas.

3

In the morning the first thing Patrick noticed when he looked out the window of the bungalow he found himself settled in with Maud and John Diver, was the mountains. They were beyond description, and far beyond anything Patrick Trainor had seen or would ever be likely to see again. He stood and stared for ages at the snow capped peaks of the highest mountains in the world, turning now and then to look away, then turning back again to make sure that they were real. He went outside to the yard at the back of the house, and had barely walked three feet, when he nearly found himself tumbling down a precipice. In fact, all of Simla was precariously perched on the sides of ravine sided hills, and it absolutely amazed Patrick how they could ever have built roads up to it in the first place. Simla was more than seven thousand feet above sea level and he found it had to believe that this was where the British Raj ruled India from between April and October. "Good morning, Pat" beamed a refreshed Maud Diver, smartly dressed in a sweet morning-grey outfit. Patrick felt very unkempt. His shirt was unbuttoned and most of his torso was exposed. He had worn the same shirt and breeches since he left ship. Fortunately, being only sixteen, he only had to shave every three or four days. He caught Maud just in time before she stepped over the precipice.
"Morning to you, Maud. How's John?" She

clung to his arm as they gazed out over Simla.

"A little better. The doctor says he has typhoid and that it was a good thing we got him out of the plains. Thank you." She stretched up on her toes and kissed him right on the lips. It was not a fleeting kiss, It lingered. Her lips did not feel the least like rubber. They were soft and wet.

"What are you thanking me for?" Her delirious husband was inside the bungalow under a mosquito net. Patrick thought that the heat and the thin air must have gone to her head to kiss him so brazenly with him in the bungalow.

"Without your help, I would never have got him here. Auntie Georgina is so relieved." She kissed him again, passionately, until he had to gasp for breath. He began to feel stiff and uncomfortable, for if either one of them lost their balance, they would pull the other over the precipice. "She wants to meet you."

"The Vicereine of India wants to meet me?" Patrick was flabbergasted. Meeting the wife of the Viceroy? Maud ran her hands over his exposed chest which weeks before had braved the Cape.

"She's Irish isn't she, and you know what the English say about the Irish - they're as thick as thieves." She spoke with a broad Mayo accent that made Patrick laugh. "I'll just go into John and then I'll take you to see her. She's playing tennis this morning." She pecked him on the cheek and went inside.

Left alone on the three feet of (literally)

yard, he began to wonder what he had got himself mixed-up in with Maud Diver. She was a strange one. Her name brought another of Tennyson's poems to mind. (India was having a strange effect on him. At school he could not remember a line of poetry to save him, but here in India, everything was flooding back to him.) There were a couple of lines from Tennyson's poem *Maud* that seemed appropriate for the situation.

> Yet, if she were not a cheat,
> If Maud were all she seemed,
> And her smile were all I dreamed...

Patrick thought the real Maud very attractive, but he doubted that she was in love with him. They'd spent three days travelling together, most of it under the searing eye of Wellesley, and the sound of Diver vomiting. He could not make head or tail of her. One minute she was coy and quiet, the next forward and opinionated. It was as if she could not accept being Mrs. Diver, the quiet demure wife. She wanted to be Maud, bold and trouser seeking. Yet, what was she really thinking? What did she mean by saying that John was not interested in her? Was it a marriage of convenience? Maybe she just felt sorry for Patrick being on his own.

> Perhaps the smile and tender tone
> Came out of her pitying womanhood,
> For am I not, am I not, here alone...

Patrick went inside to tidy himself best be

could before he met Auntie Georgina. As he passed the room in which John was invalided, he noticed the door slightly ajar. To his shock he caught a glimpse of Maud naked astride sick John Diver.

"No, princess" he was pleading, "Can't you see I'm ill."

Patrick had intended not to listen, but he lingered outside the door.

"You know how I must have it all the time. Why can't you give me what I want?"

"I can't go on like this. Get off me, Maud. Please. You're killing me." The tone of John Diver was serious. He was in pain, mental pain at having married a nymphomaniac. At first he had thought it wonderful that he had married a younger woman who never said no to sex, but he had soon learned that such a blessing, was a curse, as it had grown to dominate their entire relationship. Friends had warned him that he was being rash in marrying a girl less than half his age, but he had dismissed their warnings as envy for trapping someone so attractive and full of vitality. In hindsight, John realised that the trap had been sprung on him. In normal circles, an unmarried woman with such a sexual appetite would be viewed as a harlot, but that once married, relationships with other men would be blamed on the husband for his inability to bridle her.

"Then I'll get what I want elsewhere" she stated very clearly to her husband. It was said in a manner that made John Diver out to be the one at fault.

Patrick had heard enough. He hoped to

silently creep into his own room unheard, but a floorboard creaked, and a nude Maud Diver appeared in the corridor. She was much smaller and slimmer than he imagined. Her breasts were very small with long rubber nipples, and the rest of her figure was almost boy like. She did have beautiful slender legs and thighs, between which there was a tuft of reddish hair.

She put her finger to her lips, and led him into the room where he had spent the night.

Patrick tried to say something, but it was a feeble attempt, as her large moist lips silenced him. She pulled off his shirt and forced down his breeches, so that in the space of three days, he found himself being milked again. This time it was a white Irish woman, a protestant, so eager to find him inside her, that his breeches remained around his ankles. She did not bring him off quickly as Sita had done, for all the while he thought about her husband lying under the mosquito net next door. Try as he might to end it with a rush of life, he remained erect, to the extent that Maud began to moan louder and louder. He placed his hand over her mouth, but she bit his middle finger, and in anger he rolled her over on to her belly, and began punishing her with forceful thrusts. He had a sudden desire to use her, to teach her that he was not to be used, and as he pummelled her vigorously, her loud moans became cries.

"More! More!" she squealed.

"Jesus Christ" Patrick muttered wondering when it was going to end.

Suddenly Maud let out a loud cry and began to shudder. Patrick thought there was something wrong and eased out of her, but in an instant, she turned on her back and brought him back down on top of her.

"Don't stop. Give me more." She wrapped her arms around his neck and began licking the inside of his right ear. Patrick did not like that very much, especially as his ears were full of wax. He forced her lips on to his own, and as she began to shudder again he felt his own juice rising. At the moment of eruption he withdrew from her and laid his manhood on her perspiring belly. Even he was surprised at the quantity of the issue.

"Why did you pull out?" she asked still shaking. They were both completely drenched in sweat, and the entire room was scented with sex.

"We don't want any we baby Diver's, do we?" he said.

"Don't be silly, I've got a sponge up there. You should have asked me if it was alright" she replied.

"Oh." Patrick did not know that women did that sort of thing. His father at home in Killarney had warned him, before he had gone to Dublin, not to give a woman his sperm, unless he wanted to marry her. Patrick had reckoned his father had not included prostitutes in that statement. Patrick had not pulled out of Sita once. She had been much better at sex than Maud.

"You've done this before" Maud said kissing him gently on the lips. "You're much more experienced than I imagined." She tried to make him hard again.

Patrick was not about to tell her that he had acquired his experience over two nights in Bombay. He responded to her fingers, for he was young, and full of life.

"You're not worn out like John" she whispered "or need half-an-hour like Diarmid."

Suddenly Patrick was incensed. So Wellesley had been inside her too! That's why he was so angry on the train, he had been giving her it on the ship from Suez to Bombay and he wanted more. Well, Wellesley, thought Patrick, I got in your way; I'm giving it to her now.

He entered Maud again, thinking back to the time he had seen Wellesley in the field, pathetically trying to get it into the poor thirteen-year-old peasant girl he had raped.

*

By the time Maud and Patrick got up to Auntie Georgina's, Lady Dufferin was off the courts and back at Peterhoff, the vice regal lodge, nicknamed the 'Pig-Sty' by the previous viceroy Lord Lytton. When Patrick first saw it he thought it was a family cottage, and not the vice regal establishment.

The 'Number One Mensahib' was preparing to ride in her carriage along the main thoroughfare, when her niece and Patrick came upon her. Patrick thought her a most grand looking woman.

"Maudie, dear, I was expecting you at the courts." She spoke like one of the hunting set that lived within five miles of Windsor. She asked Maud how her husband was, then eyed up Patrick, his crinkled shirt, and his stained blue-cotton breeches.

"This is Pat, auntie."

"Pleased to meet you" she said with a certain amount of disdain. "I'd invite you into the house, dear, but I'm frightened that if one more person enters it, the weight would send the entire lot sliding down the mountainside. I'm going to persuade D that the Home Government finance a new residence immediately."

It was the Dufferin's first summer in Simla. They had arrived in India in December, and spent their first four months governing from Calcutta. Now decamped with the rest of the government to the hills, Lady Dufferin was only just getting to grips with it.

"I'd take you in my carriage, dear, but I'm afraid only D and I are allowed to ride in a carriage along the Mall. If you want to follow me to church, one of the servants will get you a rickshaw or a dandy."

At that moment, Lord Dufferin emerged from the Lodge in his Sunday attire. He was a rather average looking man, the sort you would miss seeing in a crowd, except that he was dressed lavishly, for he had to keep to the rigid hierarchical protocol expected of him as Viceroy. He took one look at Patrick.

"My God, man, have you got no-one to iron your shirt?"

Patrick felt very uncomfortable.

"Be quiet, D. That young man is a friend of Maud's"

The Viceroy got into the carriage. "Is he somebody's son?" he asked quietly, thinking that he had been too hasty in his judgment and that he had offended a Churchill or somebody.

"Not that I know of, dear. Be kind to him."

Lord Dufferin smiled benignly from the carriage. He beckoned Maud to come closer. "Sorry, I can't give you a squeeze and a hug, precious. The natives, you know." He gripped her hand resting on the carriage door.

"That's alright, Uncle D."

Jesus, thought Patrick, not him too! With her uncle? When had all that started? After the Dufferins had set off in their carriage, Patrick asked her, but she answered him with an impertinent smile that told him to mind his own business.

Instead of going to church (Patrick was Catholic after all, not Church of England), they walked to beautiful Annandale Glen with its streams and narrow mountain paths. As it was Sunday, families and groups of Anglo-Indians were already picnicking here and there beneath the trees. Those who were careless enough to leave their hampers unguarded, soon found them raided by black-faced monkeys, the original inhabitants of Simla. It was with some amusement that Patrick and Maud saw one monkey run off with the contents of an entire whicker basket, hotly pursued by two irate army officers.

As the walk continued, it was not Maud's flirtations with the men that passed them on the paths that aroused Patrick's indignation, it was the lack of civility and attention the Anglos gave to the natives. Patrick, unwilling to treat the natives as inferiors, noted that they were kept firmly in their place by the whites, made to step aside on the paths, neither greeted nor acknowledged as they were passed on by. Patrick noted this attitude of superior difference with a shock, for he had not expected to find the attitudes of the English to be a stumbling block to racial integration. Maud had noted it too.

"Have you ever thought, Pat, that natives would be more attracted to us if they were treated with kindness and firmness, but not with brutality and contempt? I can't help thinking that the English know nothing of the real character of the native."

"A bit like Ireland, then." Patrick's mother had been fighting to get the English out of Ireland all of her life. It was Vivian, if you recall, who had converted his father to the same cause. "Whether a man has a black face or a different religion, there's no need to be treated like a brute. Why is it I get the impression that the British Empire exists purely for the benefit of the English?"

They walked back down the glen to the Diver's bungalow. A servant had prepared lunch, and after they had eaten, and the servant sent away, Maud began making advances to Patrick again by rubbing her naked foot against the inside of his leg from the opposite side of the dining table.

"Don't you think you should look after your sick husband?"

"That's what the doctor is for. He said he'd pop in this evening." She had risen and walked round the dining table and sat astride him on his hard backed dining chair.

"That's not what I mean."

"You mean .... that? He's not even capable of a stiffy." The word 'stiffy' sounded menacing coming from her lips. She unbuttoned his shirt.

"I've decided to go back to Delhi."

"What for?" she replied in surprise. "I need you." She took Patrick's hands up under her skirt and past her chemise, and placed them on her inner thighs

"You don't need me, Maud. Jesus, there's hundred's of loose men running around Simla." The fingers of one hand found the slit in her drawers while the other travelled up and undid the drawstring. Her drawers fell away to expose her naked belly.

"What does that mean? Are you saying I'm an easy cunny."

"No" he lied. He pushed his fingers into the folds of her slit, sliding them past her fleshy, pouting lips.

"Well" she whispered "are you going to fiddle about with your fingers, or are you doing to do me proper?"

Patrick opened his breeches and pulled out his shaft. Maud's wet tongue came out to lick around her own mouth when she saw it. She slid her legs wider apart, and in an instant, Patrick put his member between thighs, it's head butting at the lips of her fleshy opening.

Maud put a hand between their bellies to prize open her split for him, and with a long push, he sank his length into her. She threw her head back, closed her eyes, and bucked her belly up and down in a lively rhythm. He assaulted her with short sharp jabs that made the chair creak, and within a few minutes of penetrating her, he spent copiously into her hot folds.

Maud pushed herself off his body almost before the last drop was delivered, and stood up and gave herself a perfunctory wipe with the hem of her skirt. Patrick remained on the chair, his legs a little apart, his breeches open, so that his wet and softening penis hung out in full view.

"There, you've had me again" said Maud. Suddenly something caught her attention, and Patrick turning to look, saw John Diver half-propped up against the door staring at him. He looked as white as ghost, and it was obvious he had been there long enough to see what had been going on. He turned and returned to his sick room.

Maud made no attempt to run after him. She stared out the window. Patrick did up his trousers and went to the wash-down to clean himself. When he returned, he found his small travel bag sitting on the dining table.

"I'll see you down to the Mall" she said picking up her sun-hat.

They said little to one another until they reached the main thoroughfare from which the charábancs left for the Plain.

"Ambala! Ambala!" a native shouted. "Ambala, sahib?" he asked Patrick. He nodded his head.

"See you, then" Maud grimaced.

"Aye" replied Patrick. It was all very strange to him. "Enjoy life in Simla."

Maud shook his hand. There was to be no peck on the cheek or meeting of lips in public, especially with the natives about. It all seemed so artificial and pointless, when barely half-an-hour before they had been as intimate as a man and woman could be.

"Cheerio" she said with such finality, it sounded as though he was about to die. Perhaps socially, in Simla, he had, for he got the distinct feeling that Maud Diver was happy to see the back of him, in case he became an embarrassment to her. After all, she was the Vicereine's niece, and there was no denying that the society doors of India were about to be flung wide open to her.

Patrick felt a kind of anger, perhaps the same anger Wellesley had felt at Delhi station when he realised that Maud Diver was brushing him off. Anyway, what the hell, he had six days to get to Calcutta, and Maud Diver could go to the devil.

She gave a little wave as the charábanc set off, and just for an instant, as the afternoon sun cut across the lower half of her face, he saw those large appealing lips glisten and part, then close with a smile, and he felt a little sad, and melancholic at being once more alone in the world. For he had enjoyed her company, and putting aside her infidel nature, she was a spirited girl. Buoyed by the canter of the carriage horses and the rhythm of their hooves, the words of *Maud* returned fully to him.

> Ah, what shall I be at fifty?
> Should Nature keep me alive?
> If I find the world so bitter
> When I am but twenty-five?
> Yet, if she were not a cheat,

If Maud were all she seemed,
And her smile were all that I dreamed,
Then the world would not be bitter
Maud's smile could make it sweet.

Patrick laughed. Life went on, and in India, every moment of life seemed to his sixteen year-old mind to promise the unexpected.

4

It is with some regret that we cannot tell everything of Patrick's journey through India, for such a story would require half a book to tell. However, it should suffice to say that he found time to visit the Taj Mahal near Agra, and to his dismay and disappointment, he discovered it in a sad state of repair. It is reasonable to understand that Shah Jehan's shrine to his wife Muntaz, one of the seven wonders of the modern world, had been partially plundered for materials by local builders, for it was rich in marble and mosaics. Patrick could not fault the commercial logic of this, but he little understood the British administration's lack of interest in preserving such a beautiful shrine. It was the equivalent of Britain being governed by Romans, who out of lack of historical interest, allowed the pillars of Stonehenge to be removed for building houses.
As a young man in India, Patrick saw everything in a clear light, and it angered him. The heat and the poverty he could accept, but the decay bothered him. He could not come to terms with a civilisation that was more than three thousand years

old. He never seemed to be alone. There was always someone, somewhere, watching him. There was nowhere in India to find peace, nowhere to escape the smells and noises. India was all consuming, it filled every part of his mind and occupied all of his senses. There was no escape, even in sleep, the subconscious tried desperately to unravel the sounds of the jackals or the wails of the lepers. In the light of day, dowsed with the scents of sandalwood or patchouli, nothing could mask the smell of curry, or frying eggs, or the baking of rotes. The bazaars, endless streets of wares of every kind, stretched into one another along the railway lines that ran across hundreds of miles of fields and tangled jungle as he travelled east towards Calcutta. He stopped in Cawnpore, Lucknow, Allahabad, places where the worst atrocities of the Mutiny had taken place on both sides.

In Varanasi, India's most magic city, Patrick had his first profound religious experience. The past and present appeared to Patrick to have met each other in the candle-lit, winding, narrow, scented streets of Varanasi where its people talked, ate, smoked, drank tea, and slept. He wandered the alleys between Chitganj and Andanpura Road, and by chance came upon Godaulla and the way that led pilgrims down to the Ganges *ghats*. These steps, leading down to the river, still radiated more than just gentle warmth as dusk fell. The cackling of three snow-white geese pierced the constant hum of near to distant voices and tolling bells. Small boats rocked in the wake of large river going vessels, avoiding best they could, the shaven heads of swimming pilgrims.

At the water's edge, the remains of countless pyres smouldered, each pile of ash all that was left of a loved one. Relatives bereft, wailed and cried, clung together or consoled each other, while others came to set a torch to another funeral pyre. Darkness closed in, as small sparks, then heat and light, rose from a fresh mould of wood to engulf a linen wrapped corpse. For an instant there was only the cackling of wood, and the in-rush of air to the pyre as the corpse collapsed into it. It was the point at which the spirit was released to climb high with the flakes of fire that floated star wards. It was the deceased's moment to escape the endless cycle of reincarnation. It was the point at which those watching visually saw the corpse's spirit leave the body and pass over to the other side.

Patrick was affected by it. In antipathy to his feelings about the Parsee corpses being devoured by vultures, by witnessing the cremations on the banks of the Ganges, it was his wish to be released the same way when he died, not placed in some stinking wet hole in the bogs of Ireland, to be trampled upon, dug up, or built upon. He did not relish the thought of having to claw his way out from under six feet of sod to escape his corpse. If he was going to go, he wanted to go by the Hindu method, not the Roman Catholic way of a quick shovel-full of lime to help you on your heavenly journey.

5

The *Leinster* entered the muddy estuary of the Hooghly six days after leaving Bombay. It was the final calm before the monsoon arrived. Not a breeze had ruffled the surface of the sea the entire way. The pilot brig picked them up and anchored them in the afternoon off Saugor Lighthouse to wait for the following morning's tide. At nine the next morning, they were guided up river between flat banks, dotted with palm trees and low huts.

Captain MacWhirter's thoughts were not about India itself, but had wandered into dreams of the thousands of his countrymen who had gone up the Hooghly to begin their work in Hindustan with the hope of becoming *nabobs*. So many had honour, glory, riches in their eyes, that it was sad to think that it were a much diminished number who returned down the same river. India had an unquenchable appetite, sucking men and women into her, but rarely giving them up again. MacWhirter had lost his sister at the siege of Lucknow in July '57. She'd died of cholera in the Begum Kothi, aged twenty-three.

He had put men ashore in Calcutta and Bombay, only to learn in subsequent years, that they had died of something or other, sometimes killed. It irked his Christian conscience to think that he might have saved them from such fates had he not brought them to the shores of India in the first place. In recent years the toll had not been so great, but still, the odds were fifty-fifty.

With these things in mind, he hoped for Patrick Trainor's sake, that he'd had the sense to go to the harbour-master in Bombay, and receive his instructions to meet the ship in Calcutta. He had known Tom Trainor since they were boys in Belfast, and he did not want to go home and announce to his friend that he had abandoned his nephew in India.

The *Leinster* reached its moorings opposite the Maidan about sunset, squeezed between a forest of ship's masts and black funnels. Crowds of smaller craft speedily surrounded her, and amidst a crash of coolie dockers, boatmen roaring, crew shouting and cargo whirling about, the Captain found his hand grasped by merchants welcome to receive it, and somehow or other, found himself ashore in Calcutta, and in the hospitable home of an old friend, who was the son of an older friend still.

*

Patrick arrived in Calcutta nine days after leaving Bombay; immediately, he went down to the river, and to his joy, found the *Leinster* moored there. Some of the crew greeted him like a long lost son.

"Well, if its no ra' bordello boy o 'Bombay" Gus belched at him, pinning Patrick's arms to his side in a bear hug. "Ah thought wi'd never see yer nibs again."

"You know what it takes to be a seaman, you does, Pat." Sammy was referring to the fifteen hundred miles he had travelled to get back to the ship.

"The Captain wis fair livid wi' ye fur missin' us in Bombay. But he hud to sail, we'd huv lost the pilot and hud to huv waited another three days." Gus was drunk. He had a clay jug in his hand.

"What are you drinking, Gus?"

"A'm oan ra' punch, ye know, ra' local bevvie." Punch, or *panch* had originated in Calcutta, a mixture of five ingredients - sugar, lime, spices, milk, and arrack (rice spirit).

"Where's the Captain, Sammy?"

"You know we haven't be seeing MacWhirter these three days, Pat." Sammy had a worried look, as if the disappearance of the Captain was not a normal occurrence. "It don't be like the Captain to go ashore. You better report to MacBride."

MacBride was the First Officer. He was a youngish man from Dundee.

"We're glad to have you back, Trainor." He seemed perplexed.

"I hear the Captain's missing."

"Aye, we've sent out the first mate and half the crew to find him. Get down to the galley. The cook could do with a hand."

Patrick took his orders and helped the cook prepare the evening meal. He had just being released from his duty and gone on deck to get some air, when the rest of the crew returned from shore. Johnston, the first mate, went straight to MacBride, and it was obvious from the conversation that they had not found him. The entire ship's company was assembled.

"The Captain was last seen on Ganguly Street after spending the night with one of his old merchants pals. It was presumed he was returning to the ship. Mister Johnston enquired everywhere, but no one has seen him. After supper, I'll take some of you, and we'll enquire again."

The crew was exceptionally silent during dinner. The heat was in excess of ninety degrees, and the monsoon season was about to break on them. MacBride picked out a handful of men, including Sammy, Patrick, and Gus, who after eating had sobered up. MacBride had divided the city into sections, crossing out those that had already been searched. The task was daunting. In Calcutta, there were seven hundred thousand people. In Bengal, as a whole, forty-five million!

They split into two parties. Patrick was paired with his watch; Sammy; a hand called Skerrit; a rigger called Jones; and Gus, who as third mate, was in charge of the party. They were to search the area between Bentinick Street, Park Street, Free School Street, and Bazar Street, asking here and there for Captain MacWhirter.

It was a ridiculous search, muttered Sammy, to try and find the Captain in the dark.

He was right. In Calcutta, as in Simla, Patrick was surprised to find many of the houses lit by electricity, but the light did not penetrate into the streets. They had to find their way about by carrying lanterns, and with the baying of the jackals and the whirring of bats wings, it was an uncomfortable experience. Skerrit was decidedly jumpy, and when a leper approached him and thrust a half-eaten hand out and called for *baksheesh*, Skerrit fled back to the ship.

"It's only a poor auld beggar" Gus reassured the rest "Gie him a couple o' pies."

Sammy gave the beggar, wrapped in a disintegrating brown cloth, three *piase*. The beggar went away happy. There were one hundred paise to the rupee, and Patrick realised that his five and ten rupee generosity of his first days in India, had been way beyond a native's expectation. An Indian could get by on fifty piase a day.

The area they searched was seething with nightlife. It was strung with coffee houses and eating-places frequented by well-heeled Bengalis flaunting their wealth. Fortunes were being made and lost everyday, and the city, as India's capital, was flush with money, opportunity, and corruption. Many were the sons of *zemindars*, spending the incomes of their landowning fathers, gambling it on speculative ventures, dealing with latter-day *nabobs*, using government money to line their own pockets. No one was beyond immorality; the coffee shops were the broker-houses for all the big deals taking place in India. The Viceroy and his government were up in Simla for the half-year, and without the bureaucratic department heads around, the day to day clerks were out and about negotiating personal deals.

"A'm sure one of r'ese bastards's got oor Captain" smiled the second mate.

"Why'd you think that, Gus?" Patrick asked seriously.

"Ah've been a lot o'places, son, an' Ah can tell rats fae mice." Patrick stared at Gus to see if he was sober. "Right, we're gaun'n in r'er fur a cup o' caffee."

The three seamen followed their third mate into the Indian Coffee House. It was finely decorated with wicker chairs and highly polished tables. They sat down and were served by a turbaned waiter.

"Yes, sahibs" the waiter demanded with a haughty flick of the cloth over his arm.

"Four whiskeys!" ordered Gus. Jones's face lit up. "Bet ye thought A'h was aff me nut, eh Jonesey. Ye'll no get me drinking r'at caffee shite. It gies me the runs. It's ye'r gaff."

The waiter brought the whiskeys. Jones paid.

"Have we given up looking for the Captain?" Patrick asked.

"Christ, son, dae ye think we'll find him? A've been wi' MacWhirter lang enough tae know wit he's like. He has benders, son, and serious benders. No just a wee dram. The man disnae wann't to be fund. He'll show up when he's ready."

"But three days away from the ship?" Patrick argued.

"Heavens, ye wee scunner, ye were away fur ten days wur ye no?"

Sammy and Jones laughed.

"He be right, Pat. MacWhirter'll show up when he be ready" Sammy said with the clap of a hand on his shoulder.

"Well, buoyo" Jones chipped in "that MacBride is a rookie if ever I saw one. Let's have another!"

By the time they returned to the ship, they were all roaring drunk. Patrick was in high dudgeon, trying to pick a fight with Jones, but Jones just kept slapping the back of Patrick's hands and laughing. As they boarded ship, MacWhirter appeared at the head of the gangplank.

"And where have you been, you tinkers?" he boomed.

"Ashore, Captain, sir, Officer MacBride's orders, sir" replied Gus, trying to stand in one place long enough to salute. "Permission to come aboard, Captain., sir."

"MacBride!" MacWhirter's voice shook the ship.

"Captain?" MacBride replied coming quickly on deck.

"Did you allow these men to go ashore."

"Aye, sir, but ......"

MacBride never got the chance to explain. The Captain laid into him about ship's discipline, and how, in his absence he expected his first officer to run a tight ship. He had only been gone three days, and he had returned to find no watch posted and four of the crew outrageous drunk on the quay. He said he would require an explanation in the morning.

"Get the three regulars sobered up with buckets of water, and the boy sent to his bunk."

"Aye, sir."

With that, Captain MacWhirter went below, and the next time Patrick saw him was two days later, when they had cleared the mud banks of the Hooghly and set the pilot adrift, giving the order to raise the main sheet for the homeward journey to Ireland.

Nothing was ever said within the Captain's earshot about his three-day disappearance in Calcutta, while Patrick was made to pay for his ten-day absence with an endless list of menial tasks until Dondra Head disappeared off to stern.

6

In all Patrick Trainor spent more than two years before the mast aboard the *Leinster*, until one day, shortly after his eighteenth birthday, he decided on arrival at the East India Dock, London, that it was time to quit.

He'd had enough of the sea, and having been to the East five times with Captain MacWhirter, he was ready for a quiet life on-shore. His Uncle Tom had opened up a clothing factory in London and promised his nephew a job as a junior manager, but he soon found a better position in the company as a salesman out on the road selling the company's ware. His brief was to go from store to store, but when he found the time, he liked to call door-to-door on the residencies of the rich, to try and arrange afternoon parties for the lady of the house and her society friends, so they could view his uncle's more fashionably, and expensive items.

It was on one such afternoon he took his two part-time models, Nicky and Betsy, along to a showing in Richmond. Nicky was a sweet, blue-eyed, fulsome blonde girl who thought she was Patrick's girlfriend. Unknown to her, Patrick was seeing Betsy on the side.

Carrying their fashion items, they were shown into a large drawing room where a Chinese screen had been erected for them to change behind. A dozen seats had been placed in a semi-circle some distance back from the screen.

"Right, girls, I don't want any cock-ups like the last time. If the hostess or her friends say anything bitchy about your looks, smile. Get it?" Patrick was nervous. Nicky tended to be temperamental, while Betsy, a brunette with oval green eyes and assets to match, was moody. "If we make a sale, you're on a quid each."

"And what if we don't" asked Nicky with a familiarity that Patrick detested when they were working.

"Ten bob" he replied irritated.

"Each, cock?" asked Betsy.

"Between you." Well, thought Patrick, give them too much money, and they'll start swanking it. The last thing he wanted were his models running up expensive habits. If they got their money too easy, they would think him easy, and walk all over him.

The drawing room door opened and they could hear a gaggle of voices, the clink of champagne glasses, the rustle of crinoline, and a shuffle of feet as the ladies took their seats.

"Right, let's get the show started." Patrick declared straightening his neck-tie, before abandoning the screen, to present himself to the ladies.

"He's got a brass neck" hissed Nicky to Betsy as they waited behind the screen. "I know he's screwing you?"

"Shut up, you tart" she replied under her breathe, digging her elbow into Nicky's side.

"And now, ladies" Patrick announced just as Nicky slapped Betsy across the face. Had she not stepped out with a hurried step to model, Betsy would surely have sent her flying through the Chinese screen.

"Here we have Miss Miller ...."

Thereafter the two girls were kept apart by their work, one exiting from the screen as the other entered.

The show was a success. There was one lady, a gorgeous-looking creature, who arranged for Patrick to call on her on Tuesday the following week, which by that time, she said, she would have decided on which items and what sizes she wished to order. It was only after she had left, that he glanced at her card, and with a degree of shock, discovered he had been speaking to Lady Elizabeth Shum.

*

Marion had not turned her back on the Rostov fortune after all. After shivering and freezing on the steps of Nelson's Column, she had gone to Henry James's house in Bolton Street and in the morning been coaxed to return to James Fletcher's office with Alice James to collect her inheritance. Advised by Alice, she announced that she wanted to sell all her foreign assets - the sugar plantation, the vineyard, the quarter share of the opera house, her interest in the silver mine. Fletcher said that he would see to that, but that he could not promise the best prices as the markets were slow, though he said he would do the best he could. He suggested she sell Notting Hill, that he had a buyer, but Alice James, sensing that James Fletcher was a sharp businessman hiding behind an easy smile, advised her to hold on to Notting Hill for a while.

Fletcher seemed irritated by Alice's intervention, but settled for Marion signing the necessary papers for the release of the foreign assets.

"I don't trust that man" said Alice as they travelled back to Bolton Street "His eyes are too close together." Alice James could not pinpoint exactly what it was he did not like about James Fletcher. "Knowing the sort of shady deals your father got himself into, Fletcher must know a few tricks himself. Nobody gets rich without robbing somebody else" she drolled in her New England accent.

Three years had passed since then.

Alice James had moved up the Thames to Oxfordshire attended by Katherine Loring, and was frequently visited by Marion, and by Henry, who continued to live in London scraping by on his writing earnings. Marion had bought herself a modest house in

Teddington, and with her money, had founded various charities for the benefit of orphans. The London Sisters of Our Lady were regular visitors, as was Cardinal Newman when he came to the capital. She donated vast sums to many of the Cardinal's worthwhile causes, for it seemed quite inconceivable that she would ever manage to spend more than half a million pounds in her lifetime. But in three years, her half million had been reduced to a quarter, and it was with some misgivings, she decided to give less to charities, and to spend a little more on herself. The sale of her foreign assets had mounted to a little over twenty thousand pounds. At the time Alice James had accused James Fletcher of fraud, but when challenged by his legal department, she dropped the allegation, as she had neither the proof nor the support of Marion. Thereafter, she fell into another bout of sickness, and she never quite recovered the strength that she had found to guide Marion through her first months as an heiress.

On the question of suitors, there had been a queue outside Marion's door, including the Prince of Wales, but one by one she had sent them away under some pretext or other, fawning boredom, disinterest, and even on one occasion, that she was a lesbian. In the case of Prince Edward, she cited his age, and his married status, as reasons not to see him. She was sure that her teenage relationship with Sissy was not her true inclination, for she had a desire for children, and a definite interest in men, although to date, it had been somewhat latent. Then, when she saw Patrick Trainor, how handsome he was, how confident, witty, and entertaining he had been at the fashion party, she decided that he was just the sort of man for her. To cap it all, he was Irish, and no doubt the same religion, for there was something decidedly un-Protestant about him. At first she could not decide what, then it struck her. He was not righteous. Yes, he was arrogant and at times haughty, but on no occasion was he in the slightest way condescending or adamant about his convictions that woman 'should' do this, or 'must' wear that. 'Should' and 'must' were words that would have sounded foreign coming from him. He was a 'perhaps', a 'maybe' man, words used by catholic boys, who had learned by the rigours of confession, that the rules of life were not laid down by men, but by God. Marion knew she was deluding herself about Patrick Trainor's belief in God when she showed him into her sitting room and he began to talk about how lovely she looked, and how a woman like her was made for love. It was all a bit overwhelming, for no sooner had he begun to show her the catalogue to remind her of what she had seen at the party, than he placed his hand on her lap.

"Don't you remember me?" Patrick asked. She did not look as he remembered her, but how many Irish Lady Shum's could there be?

"No" said Marion somewhat surprised by the young man's behaviour.

"I asked you to marry me in Dublin. Remember? That night, down by the quay?"

"Oh, yes" uttered Marion. She played him along to see where the conversation would lead.

"I asked you to write to me, but you never did. I've spent almost three years thinking about you." Marion edged a little away from him, but he edged along the sofa in pursuit. "I always knew I'd see you again." He attempted to kiss her, but she moved too quickly for him, and sprung to her feet.

"Mr. Trainor! What's got into you?"

Patrick looked hurt. "You don't remember do you? You probably thought it was a joke." He threw himself back on the sofa like a spoiled little boy.

"I think you've got the wrong person" Marion declared.

"You're Lady Elizabeth Sum aren't you?"

"Lady Marion Elizabeth Shum" she corrected him.

"You went to a convent school in Meath, didn't you?"

"Yes, the Sisters of Our Lady near Navan." Marion began to wonder if Patrick had gleaned the information from the newspaper and was just another one of the many cranks that had pestered her after the trial.

Patrick was having his own doubts too. There was a resemblance to the girl he had met in Dublin, but her hair was much darker, her face more beautiful than he remembered, and her breasts unquestionably smaller. Of the last thing he could not be certain, for as a young fifteen year old, Sissy Shum's breasts might have appeared to be larger than they really were.

"Are you sure you're Sissy Shum?" he asked again.

On hearing Sissy's name, everything suddenly fell into place for Marion. She looked at Patrick's face and saw it so full of genuine looking emotion; she guessed that he had genuinely mistaken her for Sissy. She took him by the hand and made him sit back down on the sofa with her. She found it difficult to bring the words to her lips.

"Sissy's dead."

"What?"

"Didn't you read about it in the papers and magazines?"

Patrick knew nothing. He had missed reading about the whole affair, for he never read newspapers, preferring instead trashy adventure novels.

"The Rostov Babies?" Marion said in an attempt to jog his memory.

It still meant nothing to him. For the first time, Marion had met a man who did not know about her inheritance.

"Elizabeth and I met in Dublin..." Patrick blurted on.

He told Marion about his time with Sissy, including the love making, for he was not prudish about such things. He knew that women liked to hear such intimate details. He found her an easy listener, and exposed far more of himself than he thought prudent to do. To his surprise she seemed to accept his confidences without judgement, to the extent that he told her what he told no one else.

"I fell in love with Sissy. She was wonderful. I still haven't met anyone else like her."

"I know." Marion felt the same way, but for different reasons. She told her own story, and how with Sissy's death, she lost her family and her childhood.

"You'll find someone-else, Patrick"

"I suppose so." he said with the downcast look of a little boy. It was this look more than anything else that women found irresistible. Without knowing what she was doing, Marion kissed him on the cheek. He blushed.

"I've embarrassed you" Marion apologised.

"No" said Patrick quickly "not at all." It was a new experience to him. He had never blushed in the presence of a woman before. He felt totally defenceless in the presence of this beautiful looking woman who did not even seem to know how beautiful she was. In the shape he was in, he would be willing to do anything to make her happy. It was a dangerous situation. He had vowed that he would not let any woman get the better of him, especially the likes of Nicky and Betsy, but sitting on Lady Shum's sofa, he felt overwhelmingly attracted to her and wished for her to kiss him again.

Marion was more than attracted to Patrick Trainor. She had designs on him. She discussed with him about his employment history with his uncle, and on confirming his breadth of knowledge of business matters (made more romantic by his two years at sea), she plainly asked:

"How would you like to come and work for me?"

Patrick was speechless. He had resigned himself to working for his uncle. It had never occurred to him that he was free to make his own choice.

"Doing what?" he asked

"My business manager. I'm desperate to have someone manage my finances."

Marion realised that she was taking a big gamble, but here was a man she had decided would do her as a husband and a father to her children. She did not even consider that she was being calculative - her finances were in a genuine mess (simply because she had more money than she knew what to do with), and at the age of twenty-four, she wanted to have children. The house was large enough for a family of eight, so there would be absolutely no necessity to move when they were married.

Patrick did not know what was going on in Marion's mind, but he remembered that Sissy had told him that she was going to inherit one hundred and fifty thousand pounds, and he assumed that this was the money that Marion needed managed.

It was a fortune! Patrick did not need to be asked twice.

"My Uncle Tom'll have a fit when I tell him" Patrick cracked.

"I'll write to your Uncle Tom" replied Marion.

Yes! Cried Patrick to himself. Here was a woman who took control to the extent that she could even keep his own family off his back.

"Are you engaged or anything like that?" Patrick inquired. He had to know.

""No" answered Marion. "Are you asking me to marry you?" she declared boldly.

Patrick could not stop himself. Something had come over him that had made him decide that Marion was the most attractive woman he had ever met. The money she possessed had something to do with it. But more than anything it was her jet black hair and her olive eyes and her beautiful perfect skin that had won him over.

"Yes" he replied without hesitation.

They sat staring at one another. Then Marion offered her hand.

"I accept"

They shook hands as if they were concluding a business deal, then sat intimately together on the sofa, as Patrick turned the pages of the catalogue, and Marion chose the items she had made up her mind to buy.

PART TWO

1

The Empress's life had been one of tragedy. She had lost her first daughter Gisela in childhood; Rudolf had committed suicide with a common little dancer; and Valerie had escaped her mother to marry and be happy. On top of that she had endured the death of Maximillan Ferdinand, Emperor of Mexico, who had been so cruelly executed by Mexican revolutionaries.

There was not a lot left in Sisi's life to be joyful about. Her forty-five year marriage to Franz Josef had been a disaster.

Since the suicide of Rudolf, Sisi had been deranged. She always dressed in black and wandered endlessly across Europe, from Corfu to England to Switzerland, anywhere she thought that she might be able to escape the voices that infected her. While in Caux, in the mountains above Lake Geneva, she wrote to Franz Josef asking him to join her there, but she knew he would not come.

"He will be too busy arranging the celebrations for his golden jubilee" she said as she gave the telegram to be sent by her lady-in-waiting Countess Sztaray. "Like always, he is always too busy in the everyday concerns of the Empire to go sightseeing with his wife."

There was no bitterness in her statement. She knew that her endless journeying was an attempt to escape from herself. So, she went down to Montreux, then on to Geneva by steamer. She was welcomed at the Hotel Beau Rivage, for the Empress was well known there, and out of character for the Swiss, they always made a fuss of her.

It was a morning of dreamy September weather, the kind of weather that suddenly comes unexpected after the last full heat of summer. She visited the Rothschild garden and was enchanted by the aquarium with its jewel-like tropical fish. She visited a music-shop where the owner demonstrated a completely new instrument - the orchestrion. This gargantuan machine played tunes from Carmen, Rigoletto, and Tannhauser. The Carmen made Sisi think of Madeira and Olive Vanya, singing and dancing at the plantation house party. The Rigoletto brought back the nightmare experience of being shunned by the Italian aristocracy in the La Scala, during her tour of Italy with Franz Josef, just before the loss of Lombardy.

"May we have the Tannhauser again" she asked the owner, not because it was the best, but rather because the tune reminded her of nothing painful.

In the afternoon, there was time to catch the streamer back to Montreux, for in Sisi's mind there was the hope that perhaps Franz Josef would meet her in Caux after all. She walked the short distance from the hotel to the quayside with the Countess Sztaray, and as they neared the steamer, a young Italian man hurried towards them. Suddenly, without warning, he leapt at her and stabbed her violently in the breast.

"Mein Gott!" shouted Sztaray. It was so

swiftly done; the Countess saw the blow but not the weapon. As the young man sped away, Sisi fell to the ground. "What has he done?" Sztaray asked the Empress.

"Nothing, nothing" replied Sisi. "Help me to my feet." The Countess got Sisi to her feet and dusted her down.

"Show me what he's done to you ..." She looked at the Empress's coat and saw a blood stain above the left breast. "Let me take you back to the hotel tout vite!"

"Nein!" she said vehemently. "I am fine. We must get to Caux ...."

Sisi would not accept Sztaray's arm. They resumed their walk towards the steamer, the Empress trying to walk erect and graceful in her usual manner. Sztaray though she saw her stagger a little, but she would not accept any help. By the time they reached the steamer, she had turned pale, and Sztaray had to help her up the gangway. She remained upright until she set foot on deck, and then sank down clutching her breast. Moments later, she was dead.

*

Luigi Lucheni was captured and charged with the murder of the Empress of Austria. He was one of those bronzed, strong and healthy individuals who had everything to live for, but who took it into his head to be a lone assassin. As an anarchist, who belonged to no party or society, and he wanted to die for his cruel act.

Needless to say, for a brief time, he was a celebrity. His name was on the front page of every major newspaper in the world. Yet, his murder of the beautiful Elizabeth had no political effect or motive, it was viewed as one of those stupid human acts that seemed pointless and utterly tragic. For many, it seemed part and parcel of the continuing downfall of the house of Habsburg. The Austrians felt sorry for their emperor, as did much of Europe. He had outlived the tragic deaths of a daughter, a son, a wife, and a brother, and he appeared to all to be a lonely, embittered ageing man, increasingly tyrannical and despotic, whose days were numbered. Few could have guessed, that Franz Josef had another twenty years of life in him, and that he would outlive his nephew heir-apparent, Franz Ferdinand, whose murder would bring the world to war in a way that his wife Elizabeth's death reduced it to tears.

2

The Trainors had gone through seven different governesses in five years, and it was becoming increasing difficult for Marion to find a girl with good background to take the job on. She had prayed for a Charlotte Bronte or the likes of a governess from a Nancy Mitford novel, but she had not been that fortunate. The last one had been something out of Thackeray's *Vanity Fair*.
Marion had hopes for Miss Brook, she seemed well spoken, polite, and well read. Although she was not a catholic, she nevertheless had been disciplined in an orphanage, and as an orphan herself,

Marion knew what it was like to be alone in the world.

However, Marion was circumspect about this too, since Miss Pinhorn, the governess before Miss Brook, had been an orphan. She had caused no end of bother between Marion and her husband, for she was still very young for her age in some ways, though she was twenty-two. Marion had no suspicions when Patrick began to be particularly attentive and affectionate to May Pinhorn. She thought he was being kind and rather boringly fatherly to the young governess. But it embarrassed her, when he took the young lady to a shop and bought her a beautiful dress and she responded by making advances to him. At this juncture, Marion had become ill during a pregnancy and had gone to Brighton for a rest, leaving Mrs. Bradford the housekeeper in charge of all the domestic affairs. Through Mrs. Bradford, it was reported to her that Patrick spent his evenings with the young governess. By turns, amused and teased by her, he went to great lengths to appear young and active. When out for a walk with the children, he even took Miss Pinhorn's hand to help her over a stile, and she, after hearing of his exploits as a seafarer rounding the Cape, cruelly made him jump from the stile so that he twisted his ankle. Moreover, the worst was still ahead.

One Sunday afternoon, after Marion had returned fit and well to the house in Teddington, she saw from her bedroom window that faced on to the large garden at the rear of the house, Patrick and the wicked little governess in the summerhouse. She could see that they were arguing, and that she had thrown him off after he had tried to take her in his arms. She had no idea what they were arguing about, but she suspected that the girl was just making a show, for she soon gave into his advances, and had one of the children not run into the summer house at that juncture, they would have kissed.

Marion knew that Patrick had taken many mistresses in their twelve years of marriage. He had openly admitted it on two occasions. The first was a common little waitress he had met in a tea-shop in the Strand; the second, a woman called Maud Wellesley who he said he had first met in the 80's in India. Marion suspected that he was still having an affair with her, for when she brought her name up, he would stiffen and become defensive. That was not his normal nature when she asked him about other women, usually he would shrug his shoulders, or tease her, or tell her to mind her own business. But with Maud Wellesley, there was always a sense of mystery and intrigue, as though all the love that Marion deserved was being rationed to her, the best of it being kept for the Wellesley woman. It hurt, it hurt so much that Marion could not cope with it any more. She had to do something, so she sacked May Pinhorn. Patrick was furious.

"What's got into you? The children adore her!"

"It's you who adore her. The children can

get another governess. I'm not having your prostitute in my house."

Nothing more was said. The child Marion was expecting was born premature, and the subsequent death, sent Patrick into a fit of remorse. It was he who suggested that they should go to Ireland for a while. He knew their marriage was on rocky ground, and that it was up to him to prove to Marion that he still loved her.

Marion, for her part, was weak from the loss of the child, and if anything, was ready to accept love from any quarter. At the age of thirty-six, she was starting to feel old, more so, because Patrick was six years younger and still did not have a grey hair in his head. She had not foreseen the difficulties that the marrying of a younger man would bring. At the time of their marriage she could not have dreamt that he would go off with other women. She did not understand what made him like that, except that it was in his nature, inherited from his mother no doubt. Marion had always blamed herself that she could not satisfy Patrick, but as the years had gone by, she had become increasingly wanton and interested in sex, while he had become boring and disinterested. How could the cause be her? She had not allowed herself to become slovenly or fat, she had maintained her figure by regular exercise and beauty treatment, and after childbirth, had always gone to Brighton, or Bournemouth to regain her health and body shape.

Patrick, by contrast, had done no exercise

at all since his time at sea. At the age of thirty, he was still as handsome as he ever was, but from the neck down there was a general sagginess pulling him earthwards. He was still as glib-lipped as ever, charming his way through life with a silver tongue. He had managed to spend nearly all of Marion's fortune, and had she not removed him from the management of what was left of it, he would have spent that too. The various business ventures that he had persuaded Marion to invest her money in had all collapsed, not because they were under capitalised, but rather because Patrick mismanaged them. The fashion house, the hair salon, the restaurant, and finally the theatre, were all absolute flops. Patrick was always too fully committed to business and buyers meetings to get down to the every day graft of making money by watching where it came from and whom it went to. Half his time was spent chasing models, coiffeurs, waitresses, and actresses, telling them what he could do for them if he divorced his wife and married them instead. Many of these women had been taken in, but the smart ones saw that Patrick's wealth was his wife's and not his own, and that without his wife, Patrick was penniless. Nevertheless, he was a successful lover, for although many of Patrick's conquests knew that he was a liar and cheat, deep down they wanted to believe that he was in love enough with them to leave his wife and marry them.

The one exception was Maud Wellesley. She had returned to England after three years

in India with her second husband Diarmid
Wellesley. How these two had got together
again was a mystery to Patrick, but he
knew they deserved each other. He had no
love for Diarmid Wellesley, and he rather
enjoyed the thought that he was making a
cuckold out of him. Wellesley had got
himself elected to Parliament, no doubt
through the influence of the Dufferins, and
Patrick took great delight in frolicking with
his nymphomaniac wife while his rival sat
through all nighters in the House. Maud,
however, always had Patrick at her bidding,
to the extent that Patrick began to wonder
if he was being played with. He knew Maud
had a stream of men, and she had
suggested that she'd once had four men on
the same day, and that he was the fifth. He
had laughed it off, but later he began to
fear, that because of Maud Wellesley's
promiscuity, he might contract syphilis.
That was a few years before. Maud was
slowing down. She could not get the same
number of men any more as she was in her
early thirties. Time was starting to show on
her face, and her body had been so used, it
was showing signs of wear. She no longer
smelt as sweet as she used to, her
chocolate-box prettiness and reddish-
blonde curls had been replaced by a plump
face and dyed strawberry-blonde hair tied
up in a bun. She still had her blue eyes,
though they were a bit narrower than
before. The only feature that the years had
not diminished was her large rubber-like
lips that had kissed a thousand men. It was
these that Patrick returned to time and time

again, long after her more erstwhile lovers
had abandoned her for younger game. She
still had a number of lovers who would call
on her when they were in town, but it was
Patrick that she now began to wait for, to
perfume for, to think about in her spare
moments. Fifteen years had passed since
their first meeting in the Victoria Terminus
in Bombay. Fifteen years she had been
married to Wellesley who had shown up at
John Diver's funeral in Simla, and proposed
to her the following day. He had caught her
off guard. She had forgotten his bad
manners, and remembered only the nights
of sex they'd had, on the steamer from the
Red Sea to Bombay, while her husband
slept. Now she fully knew him to be the
bastard that others had told her he was.
After years of asking Patrick to tell her what
the grudge was between him and her
husband, she had discovered that Patrick
had seen him rape an Irish peasant girl.
She then told Patrick that Wellesley had
been accused of the same thing in India,
with a native girl, but that he had denied it,
and got off scot-free. However, the scandal
had forced them to return to England. At
the time Maud had wholehearted believed
in Wellesley's innocence, but now she knew
better.

If nothing else, the knowledge of the
animosity between Patrick and her husband
added fuel to the love affair she continued
to have with Patrick Trainor. The hatred
they had for one another was like an
aphrodisiac to her. She was their go-
between, for despite her disdain of her

husband, it did not stop her from having sex with him, knowing as she did, that he had raped at least two women.

Patrick needed a break from the sordidness of his affair with Maud. The other girls came and went. May Pinhorn was just another affair. He had made the advances on her. She was young and naive, and it had not taken him long to have her. However, having her under the same roof as his wife was a complication he had not foreseen, and it was with some relief, that Marion sent the little governess packing. At times like that it was Marion who saved Patrick from himself. He knew that Marion was the best thing that had ever happened to him. She had given him four beautiful daughters, and despite having squandered nearly all of her inheritance, she had never rebuked him for it, believing in the will of God, and believing that one day he would see the light and find in her everything that a man might ever want from a woman.

*

It is strange how childhood memories can blend to become one full day, for Olive Trainor was almost five years old when news of Empress Elizabeth's death reached her mother. There was a good deal of excitement about the house when Nurse Hardy arrived, and Olive saw her mother cry. To her surprise, her father moved into the spare bedroom across the passage from her mother's room. Her sister's thought it odd, but Olive did not bother any more about it, until next morning when Nurse

Hardy brought a new baby boy and they were all taken to see it. There was a lot of talk as to what name he should have, but Olive's father decided that like all Trainor boys, he would be called Patrick.

Next day the baby died, and this time, the loss was so great, everybody cried. Her father and mother went to Ireland to visit Grandpa and Grandma Trainor, and Olive and her three sisters were left in the charge of Nurse Hardy, a Somerset woman, full of superstition. She warned them about sheep.

"If on your daily walk, dears, you'se see a flock of sheep and they be going away from you, then all is well. But, ifs you should meet a flock of sheep coming you'se way, you had better turn home rights away or it be very unlucky." It was an old wife's tale, but Olive had decided that she would never go for a walk in the country. "An whats if you be setting the table and two spoons accidentally lay on the table together, well, that means an engagement to marry."

Hardy had all the qualities of a witch, though to look at her, a stout, jovial thirties-something woman with a pleasant round face, she looked like a child-nurse, not a banshee. Phyllis, Cecily, and Chloe all giggled at her strange ways, but Olive listened with great seriousness to every word she uttered.

"See, dears, two knives crossed on a table means a certain quarrel, unless yous remove the top one." The old nurse grinned through her broken teeth. "If you curtsey to the moon eight times, you'll get your wish.

An as sure as anything, if you'se be bad,
the Devil will get you."

Olive was tired of being threatened without
seeing the Devil. She wanted to see him for
herself. "Does he really have horns?"

"Well, child, if you go into your mama's
bedroom when dusk 'as fallen and look into
the mirror, you'll see him lookin' over your
shoulder. You'll recognise him by the big
goat's horns he has."

Olive was determined to try and see him.
That evening, just as the lamp had been lit
in the parlour, she crept out, went up the
long winding stair to her mother's bedroom,
and shaking with fear, went in. She got
halfway across the room when she was
overcome with terror and fled back
downstairs to the warmth and light of the
parlour. She did not say a word to Hardy,
nor her sisters, and never tried to see the
Devil again.

Although Nurse Hardy was an interesting
character and a good nurse, the Trainors
were naughty children and she did not have
an easy time while Patrick and Marion were
away. As a result, when Olive's parents
returned from Ireland, Nurse Hardy left to
get married to a tall, thin man who always
dressed in black, wore a very crushed tall
hat, and was the assistant to the local
undertaker. The children went to visit her
from time to time in her new home, but not
long after, she took ill, and passed away.

The next thing Olive remembered, her
mother had engaged a governess called
Miss Brook. She was nineteen, and her
father had been killed on active service in

Africa when she was very young. Her
mother had died soon after and she had
been brought up in a home for Army
Officers' orphans where she had remained
until she was old enough to earn her own
living as a governess.

Though the children were very fond of
Brooky, as they called her, she was very
strict. She was not as nice looking as Pinny,
who had left without saying goodbye, but
she laughed a lot more, and did not shout
at them. She made little jokes about this or
that, but if any of them were rude or
spiteful, she punished them. She was
always telling them about men who built
bridges or explored jungles, but she would
never allow them to play house, or hide and
seek. Because her own childhood had been
interrupted by the death of her parents, she
had no notion of play. To her, a child's life
was a serious time of preparation for the
moment of going out alone into the world.
Without family, Brooky did not know that
children did not have to be adults in little
bodies nor that grown adults would always
be children in the eyes of their parents.

Olive could not wait to get into the
schoolroom that was next door to the
study. Although she had been allowed to
see what was in the schoolroom, she had
never been present when her sisters had
been schooled by Pinny or Crummy
Carmichael, the previous governess to her,
who on account of washing Chloe's mouth
out with soap, was sent away.

Olive remembered her first lesson quite
well. She could still see the copybook with

the lines beginning with strokes and the light blue letters printed faintly, over which she had to copy. As time went by she had produced good letters, for some years later her mother showed her some of her copybooks that she had kept.

Brooky attached great importance to the way the children held their pens. She kept a long brown wooden ruler by the side of her, even during meals. If one of the children held her pen in the wrong manner, or rested her hands on the dinner table while eating, the ruler would appear in a flash and be brought down on her knuckles. As a result of this, later in life, Olive would on occasion find her own hands resting on the table, and instantly withdraw them.

Brooky also had other methods of keeping the Trainor girls disciplined. She would at all hours of the day wear a thimble on one of her fingers, and when they were not sitting up straight enough, rap them on the head. If they misbehaved, they were often whipped. At first, Olive had gone to her mother to cry, but she soon discovered that her mother was in favour of thimbling and whipping. She'd had such trouble bringing the children into line, she had concluded that her children needed punished, and that the governess was the one for the job. After all, at the convent school in Ireland, Marion had been regular whipped *supra dorsum nudam* while tightly strapped to a bench during the castigation. Of course, she had no knowledge that her own mother Olive Vanya had been regularly flayed in Turkey. We cannot deny with certainty that acceptance of whipping had become hereditary in their family.

Although Olive was often whipped, she never resented being punished except when she considered it unjust. On one occasion when out walking, she was looking for chestnuts and lost the rest of the party. They hid from her, then went home by a different route. Olive returned home to find that everyone had been back some time. She knew she was in trouble for dallying and went straight to Brooky's room.

There was nothing much to see in the room but a plain bedstead and a toilet table with very little on it. Miss Brook was sitting at the window reading a book.

"I'm sorry, Miss Brook, I didn't mean to get lost."

"I am sorry and I did not mean, Olive Trainor. Do not use slang in my presence."

"I am sorry, Miss Brook" she started again "I did not mean to get lost. I was only collecting chestnuts for Papa."

"Very well, Olive, I accept your apology" replied Brooky without putting down her book. "But this will not let you off being punished. You must at all times stay with the party. You are not David Livingston." She put down her book, picked up the dreaded ruler, and gave Olive a good number of strokes on her bare bottom.

Olive left Miss Brook's furious. She felt it utterly wrong that they had hidden from her. She considered it unjust that she had been tricked and punished at the same time. She went to Mama, but Marion said that she had agreed not to interfere with how Miss Brook schooled them, as Miss Brook was the first governess they had employed who made them do as they were told.

From that time, Olive began to grow distant from her mother. Cecily was her favourite, for she would listen to Cecily's complaints, and speak to Miss Brook about them. Phyllis was big enough to stand up for herself, but Chloe and Olive had to suffer in silence.

Miss Brook taught them all sorts of needlework - sewing, hemming, running, backstitch, herring bone, cross-stitch, how to gusset, to mitre, do blanket stitch, button-holes, crewel work, French knots, darning, fine tucks, gathering, as well as all sorts of knitting and crochet stitches - for they had to darn their own stockings and mend their own clothes. They made handkerchief-sachets, nightdress cases, and embroidered tray clothes as presents. Even at an early age, Olive had learned to work on canvas and make kettle-holders, and despite the Trainors being an affluent household, they made all their own sheets, and spent long afternoons hand-sewing hems and joining the sides to middles of old sheets.

Olive always enjoyed these afternoons very much, for their mother would sit with them doing crewel work, making wonderfully beautiful Tudor-pattern panels for the doors between the dining room and drawing-room. They would sit there until evening waiting for their father to come home, rushing to him as he came through the door, helping him to take off his coat.

In Olive's mind, her father was like God, while her mother was like Jesus. Her father was all-powerful and knowing, he gave orders that had to be obeyed, and sometimes he shouted, and the house shook. Like Jesus, her mother never shouted and loved her no matter whatever she did, though her mother liked to be obeyed too. She felt that while she had to wait for God to come, Jesus was always with her, and at night when she cried, it was Jesus' name she would call, not God's. For at night, she was frightened of many things; she imagined trees talking and buildings moving, and once when an owl came to live in a nearby tree, it took her almost a month to accept that it was not the Devil. She had bad dreams about horses pursuing her, until she learned that if she lay down, their legs would fall off and the horses would change into sheep.

Next to her mother and father, her sisters were the most loved persons in her life. More than the others, she adored Chloe. She was two and a half years older than Olive. She had jet-black hair and dark skin and the most enormous laugh in the world. She was always on the rocking horse and would let Olive ride with her, then try to buck her off over the horse's head. It was brilliant fun!

Phyllis and Cecily were boring by comparison. They spent all their time together playing or fighting, and did not seem to have much time for Olive unless they were in a teasing mood. Olive was not as fond of them as Chloe, until one day,

sitting on the garden lawn, Phyllis placed a daisy chain around her neck and said
"We will always be together." It was one of those wishful childhood statements that one child makes and forgets, while the other never does and spends the rest of her life making come true. "We are not alone, we are us"
Olive was deliriously happy that her ten-year-old eldest sister had finally accepted her. Next day, Phyllis went away to boarding school, and Olive could not bear it until she returned home for the holidays. Olive was so eager to meet her sister that she tumbled down the stairs and landed on her chin. There was some blood, and Phyllis hated the sight of blood, but she wiped away her little sister's tears, and then gave her an enormous hug. Thereafter, it did not matter to Olive that Phyllis spent nearly all the rest of the holiday with Cecily, and sometimes Chloe, for in her mind they were all together.
Olive shared a double room with Chloe. When Cecily went off the boarding school, Olive was moved into Phyllis and Cecily's old room, with the understanding that she was to move back to share with Chloe during the holidays. But it did not work out like that. After some difficult weeks settling in and getting used to sleeping alone, Olive decided to make her sister's room her own. Day by day she removed Cecily's simple little treasures to a cupboard in the hallway, so that by the time they came home for the holidays, Olive had placed her own little objects scoured from the garden,

walks, her mother and father, grandpa and grandma, Brooky, Miss Bradford, Nurse Hardy, and placed them in such an array where Cecily's used to be, that Cecily took one look at it and immediately flew in rage and knocked all the things to the floor. She did it with such bad temper, that any sympathy she might have had was completely lost. Brooky, although Cecily was her favourite, gave her a good whipping, and she was sent to share with Chloe. Phyllis protested that she wanted to share with Cecily, not her little untidy sister, but a stern look from Brooky was enough to settle the matter. By the end of the holidays, the whole incident had been forgotten, and Cecily hinted that she was glad she did not have to suffer Phyllis's snoring any more. Phyllis, in defense, said she did not miss the rancor of Cecily's smelly feet. Chloe and Olive looked at one another, and agreed in secret, that during the next vacation, they would return to sharing as neither of them snored or had smelly feet.

*

At this juncture it must be said that Marion's life with Patrick was not a particularly happy one. She had tried corresponding with her half-brother in Turkey, but after a few years, the correspondence ceased, and she felt alone in the world.
Marion was seriously religious. She was a great admirer of Mr. -, a well-known orator, and went to see him preach. They became

firm friends and he became a regular visitor to the house. However, over a period of time, he managed to elicit a number of large donations from her, and had Patrick not put a stop to it, he would have bled her dry. Patrick forbade her from ever seeing him again, but against his wishes, she did occasionally stand in the crowds in Hyde Park just to listen to Mr. -'s voice.

Marion conducted prayers before breakfast at which the children had to sing hymns, accompanied by the harmonium. She took the whole family every Sunday to church in Richmond. She seldom took them to the local parish church, preferring instead the ceremony and trappings of the High Church. On special feast days such as Good Friday they would go to Southwark Cathedral. The Archbishop rarely preached less than an hour, and Marion loved every second of it while the children humbly held their heads and fidgeted in penance.

Marion taught the children to deny themselves something during Lent. She provided large biscuit boxes, and very morning the children deposited their lumps of sugar allowed for their breakfast into the tin boxes. At the end of Lent, Marion weighed the tins, and the money saved on sugar was given to the Kingston Orphanage.

She would not allow the children to play games on Sunday. The governess was always given the day off, and when old enough, the children were sent, sometimes with their father, to walk to Richmond Park or Hampton Court and back while Marion went to bed to sleep. In the evening Marion played the harmonium and the whole family sang hymns together.

Yet, Marion was not happy. She had looked upon Patrick as one of the truly good men that she had known. He was exceptionally kind, full of fun with the children, and had the ability to tell them stories better than anyone else. He seemed to know every man, woman and child in Teddington. He talked to all and sundry, emitting friendly greetings as if to cheer up a world that was permanent depressed. He would sit next to someone on the train or a park bench, and within minutes he would have his or her whole life story. He was a straight, upright, honest Irish gentleman who took people at face value and never disliked anyone. He was a happy man.

Consequently, Marion was unhappy because he cared for the world more than her. He had his parents in Killarney, his Uncle Tom in Dublin, his mates from his seafaring days, and Maud Wellesley. She, by contrast, had no one to reply on except him. She had put too much into the marriage, concentrated too much on the children, and had failed to make any lasting friendships with her own sex. It embarrassed her to think that Emily Brooks was the closest thing she had to female friendship. How could it even be anywhere close to what she'd had with Sisi in the convent?

Marion would meet Henry James at Sissy's grave every year on the anniversary of her death. She and Henry had paid for a modest new headstone in the pauper's cemetery and inscribed upon it 'In Memory of a Loving Sister and Daughter - Sissy Blum James, Born Dublin 1862, Died London 1883. Friends are Forgotten, Family is Forever.'

After tending the grave and laying flowers, Marion and Henry would go for tea to the Savoy Hotel where they would visit the room where Sissy had been died, then over tea, catch up on news. Henry had become quite successful and bought himself a fine house near Rye, Sussex. His sister Alice had died in '92 and he was very much alone apart from his artistic friends. He had told Marion that he much preferred men to women, but he did not go into detail about it. What he did in private was his affair, particularly after the hullabaloo about Oscar Wilde.

"They are going to release Clarissa, Henry." Marion had been visiting Clarissa in the mental institution every six weeks for seventeen years.

"When?"

"In two months. They've had her on some new medicines over the last few years and her schizophrenia is completely under control as long as she takes the drugs."

"You've been like a daughter to her" Henry said guiltily. "I, by contrast, have done nothing for her. I last visited her about twelve years ago. Where will she stay?"

"With me"

"What about your husband and the children? Won't they mind?"

"It will be another grandmother for the wee

ones. They have hardly ever seen their grandparents in Ireland. They live in their tumble down castle in Killarney and never think of coming over to England. Patrick's mother is set against the English and blames them for all of Ireland's troubles. His father is a bit wiser, but he's too busy in the courtroom with murders and the likes to tear him away. I think in all, they've maybe seen the children twice or three times. They've never seen my youngest Olive at all. I should have taken her the last time we were over with Patrick, but I'd just lost my baby, and I wasn't thinking right. Anyway, they adore their Great Uncle Tom, he comes to visit us every time he's in London."

Henry had a picture of the Trainor family as the Victorian ideal. He had not been to her home since she was married, but he could remember the great big old house with high ceilings and floral wallpaper. In those days he had always thought of her as the poor little rich girl living all alone in a draughty mansion watching the plaster crumble. But now, mature, exquisitely beautiful, immaculately dressed, he could only picture her as a great society lady.

"Do you ever use your title?" Henry asked her.

"Never" Marion replied. The thought of calling herself Lady Elizabeth made her laugh. "I don't think my mother's title was ever real, do you?" There had been considerable speculation after Sisi Blum's murder that the Rostov title was a bogus one, for a Russian émigré had written into

The Times to say that he had worked for the real Count Rostov as late as '80, and that he was alive and well and living in his castle on the Don.

"Who knows? As an American I hate titles, but at the same time, I wish I had one because they can be very useful."

He pointed to a waiter bowing and scrapping and at the same time attempting to wipe some cream cake from the lap of someone Henry recognised as Lord Dufferin. They both laughed.

"See, do you think that poor waiter would do that for any old Dufferin if he wasn't a Lord?"

"So is that Lord Dufferin?" Marion whispered with great interest. Henry nodded. "Does he have a niece called Maud?" She wanted Henry to gossip about her.

"God, yes. She's married to a toe-rag called Wellesley. He's a minister in the Colonial Office. They've sent him out to South Africa to talk to Kruger and try and settle this Boer thing."

"What's wrong with Wellesley?"

"What's right with him? Every now and then life throws up a complete and utter bastard. His grandfather was Wellington, and we all know what Wellington did for Britain. But Wellington was a bastard too, though he managed to hide it. Wellesley can't. He's mean, spiteful, and unbelievably arrogant. I've heard it said he wants to be Prime Minister. God help us if that ever comes about."

Marion heard Patrick talk the same way

about Wellesley, but she was more interested in his wife.

"And what about Missus Wellesley?"

"Maud Wellesley is no better. She must have bedded ever member of the cabinet by now."

"You mean ...?"

"I mean whatever you can imagine, she's done it. How do you think Wellesley got the Colonial Office job? Pillow talk. That's how it's done these days with Salisbury's Tories. A quick whisper in the ear of the Colonial Secretary ....."

Despite Marion's religious demeanour, she was no prude. "I did not have four children without learning something about pillow talk, Henry. There has be more to it than that?"

"Well, there is. Wellesley's the Prime Minister's nephew."

"There we have it, then" said Marion "Blood will always win out, don't you think?"

"I never under-estimate the power of sex" replied Henry "It's a woman's greatest weapon."

All the way home, Marion thought about what Henry James had said. She had never denied Patrick his rights to her; she had never used it as a means of punishing him for his unfaithfulness. When he returned home after being with another woman, she did not shun him; she embraced him, and let him make love to her so she could discover what he had learned. By taking him in her arms, she forgave him for his sins, held him like a repentant wayward son returned to the breast of his mother. Thus, she had made their marriage survive, made it more than just a sham, loved him, so that he could find no-one else to love him like she did.

By doing so, she now realised she had used sex to keep him from wandering further than he did. Sex purified him, made him happy, made him home loving and fatherly. For her own part, she enjoyed having his arms around her, having the small of her back lightly caressed by his fingers, having his manhood inside her, for at those moments he was hers, and hers only, and she would cling to him with her arms around his neck and kiss him on the neck and whisper that she loved him. Yet, all those years, she had never thought that it was sex he wanted from her. She tried to remember. The years had passed and she had convinced herself that he had married her for her money, but jogged by the rattle of the carriage across the gaps in the tracks, she recalled that he had known nothing about her money when he had first met her. She had married him because she had fallen in love with him from the moment she first saw him, but she did not consider that he had married her for the same reason.

By the time she alighted from the train at Teddington and Bushey station, she had decided that she was tired of being unhappy in her marriage. With the information she had from Henry James, she felt confident enough to confront Patrick and issue him with an ultimatum. He either promised not to see Maud Wellesley ever again, or she would go public and name Maud Wellesley as an adulteress, and drag her into court as a respondent in divorce proceedings. Then Henry reminded her that the law as yet did not permit a wife to divorce her husband, though there was talk of change.

Yes, Henry, thought Marion, sex was a woman's greatest weapon, and it's deadliest when used against another woman. She would find another way of getting rid of Maud Wellesley.

*

Grandma Clarissa came to stay the same week Queen Victoria was on her deathbed. Everyone prayed for the Queen to live, none more earnestly than Olive, but she died just the same. Everyone wore black clothes or black armbands.

No one had told Grandma Clarissa, so Olive marched boldly up to her.

"The Queen is dead!" she said.

Clarissa looked at the little eight-and-a-half year old girl. "Who are you?" she asked.

"I'm Olive, Grandma."

Clarissa began to cry. A tear rolled down one of her cheeks.

"What's the matter, Grandma? Did you know the Queen?"

"No, no" Clarissa snivelled "it's got nothing to do with that at all." Hearing the name Olive after so many years had upset her. Marion had told Clarissa that she had named one of her daughters Olive, but she had forgotten.

"Grandma, Mama says we are going to

Scotland for our holidays this summer. Can you come?"

"Oh, you will have to ask your mother, dear, she might want me to stay here." Clarissa was sixty-one, and after seventeen years in a mental hospital she could do very little for herself. She could just about eat and go to the toilet alone, but beyond that she had been institutionalised for too long, she had lost the ability to think for herself. He had become so used to decisions being made for her, she automatically left them to others.

Olive returned. "Mama says you can come if you want to come. Do come!"

"Well ..." Before Clarissa had the chance to think about it any more, Olive threw her arms around her neck and gave her a big kiss. The show of affection filled Clarissa with emotion.

"Don't cry, Grandma. We'll get another Queen, won't we?"

The sixty-four year old Victorian age had ended, and the Edwardian period begun.

"A king, liebling. Your Grandma met him when she was young."

Olive was excited by the news. "Was he your boyfriend, Grandma?"

"Nein" she laughed. Olive laughed with her.

"I love you, Grandma" Olive said snuggling into Clarissa.

"I love you too, my little darling Olive."

*

Patrick had not taken it too kindly when he heard that Clarissa was coming to stay at the house, but it was nothing compared to the ultimatum Marion delivered about Maud Wellesley, some weeks after speaking with Henry.

"Jesus, Mari, you don't believe I would go behind your back with the likes of her, do you?"

"I know you, Pat. And I've heard all about Maud Wellesley. Half the government wives in London would like to see her burnt at the stake."

"She's no witch! She's a woman with needs."

"And what sort of needs is that, then, Patrick Trainor?"

"I mean … she's popular." Patrick was getting himself into a twist.

"She must be more popular than the Albert Hall. More men have passed through her than a night at the Proms."

"You can't talk about Maud like that."

"Is she your wife? More shame on her that her husband is in on it with her."

"What do you mean by that?"

"What's she had from you, Patrick? How much has it cost me?"

"What are you talking about?"

"You can't tell me that the bitch is letting you in her trap-door without it costing you something?"

Patrick froze. A sudden look of terror filled his face. He turned away.

"Look at me!" Marion demanded. "It's too late to hide your face now! Tell me the truth!" Marion was angry, and when Marion got angry, Patrick knew better than to ignore her.

"Alright, I'll tell you! But do you promise

not to send me away."

"I'm promising nothing until I hear the truth."

"Then I won't tell you."

"Pat!" Marion shouted in despair "if you don't tell me now, it's over, you can back your bags for your mother's." Marion began pulling his shirts out of his dresser, throwing them on to the bed. He tried to stop her. In a fury, she opened the large wardrobe, and threw his suits on the floor.

"Mari! Stop it! Please!." He tried to close the wardrobe.

"Tell me!" she screamed.

Patrick sat down on the bed. "I've been seeing Maud for years, you know that. I wanted to give her up when Olive was born, but she's been blackmailing me."

"Blackmailing? What do you mean?" Marion sat down on the bed beside him a state of shock.

"She said she'd tell you what I'd done."

Marion did not want to ask, but she knew she had to. "Done what?"

"Fathered her child." Marion stared in disbelief. "He's about the same age as Olive."

Marion's mind was racing. He had been sleeping with her at the time Olive was conceived? She tried to recall, but she could not. Yes, now she remembered. It was during that period of wild sexual activity when he would come home and make love to her for half-an-hour at a time without expending himself. She knew that there had been something troubling him, but he had satisfied her so fully, she took what he gave her without asking any questions. Olive had been the consequence of his torrid attention, and now she discovered that he had got Maud Wellesley pregnant at the same time.

"I've been paying her a lump sum every month for the last nine years to keep her quiet. She never lets me see the boy, she's frightened he'll suspect something and tell Wellesley."

Marion still could not quite believe what she was hearing. "How do you know he's yours?" she asked, looking for a way out of the mess.

"I don't" Patrick said in a way that made Marion take heart.

"What do you mean?"

"I've only got her word for it. I haven't been paying her two hundred pounds a month to protect myself, I've been doing it to protect you from the truth."

"Two hundred pounds!" The thought of that amount of money being drained from the family over nine years appalled Marion. She knew her sums - it was in the region of twenty thousand pounds.

"Jesus, Mari, I've been an eggit, so I have. The English are sly bastards. I'm sure she and Diarmid Wellesley have been playing me for a sucker all along, so help me." Patrick was at his wits end. He was almost in tears.

Marion was at a loss. Patrick began crying on her shoulder and she had no desire to force him away. She felt that he deserved some severe punishment, but it was not in her heart to inflict it upon him. He had broken down and told her the truth and it was up to her now to forgive him. What was her option? He was the father of her children, and although his business ideas never seemed to succeed, he did genuinely try to make them work. Apart from the odd lapse, he was a caring husband. Perhaps now his days as a womaniser were over, and that to reject him because of the scheming ways of another woman was wrong. No, she would stick by him as she had always done, for despite his flaws, she loved him passionately.

"We're all human, Pat." She stroked his hair, which in the gaslight she saw for the first time signs of grey. "Woman can be far more evil than men, Patrick. Maud Wellesley is to be pitied. She has a husband none has a good word for, and from accounts, she is insecure and lonely. Why else would she sleep with so many men? Women do not do that sort of thing solely to advance the careers of their husbands. Perhaps in a more just society where woman have emancipation, she could channel her sexual energies for her own advancement, but in our own times that is impossible, a woman must live through her husband. I have had offers to sleep with men, many of them by rich and handsome men, but I have refused them because I am committed to you. What kind of relationship can a husband and wife like the Wellesley's have? Deceit. Mistrust. Jealousy. Recrimination. Hatred. Can they possibly love one another? If they do, then it is a perverted love that feeds on wickedness and cruelty. How can they bring up a child in such an atmosphere of evil? Tomorrow, I'm going to see the child for myself. One look and I will know if it is yours."

The boldness of Marion's last statement made Patrick lift his head from her shoulder. He looked into her eyes, her deep olive-coloured eyes. When had other men tried to entice her to sleep with them? From the way she said it she was not lying. Henry James? The preacher? No, neither was rich nor handsome. Then who? Perhaps now was the wrong time to ask, it was something to think about. He had never considered that his wife would find other men attractive; she had always been so totally devoted to him. Perhaps he had neglected her, left her too much on her own. Perhaps there was time to remedy that. One thing for certain, now was not the time to argue or protest. At times like this, Marion was in charge of their relationship and she would do what had to be done to keep them together. He knew he needed to be guided by a good woman, as his mother had guided him as a boy, to keep him on the straight and narrow path. Maud had led him a pretty dance since that day in Simla she had packed his small travelling bag, put it on the dining table, and walked him down to the station. Now, the matter was out of his hands. The two woman who had most influenced his adult life were about to do battle.

*

Marion sent her man over to Belgravia to

make the last of his enquiries. At midday, she met him at Speaker's Corner in Hyde Park to confirm that the information he had gathered was correct. Thereafter, Marion took a hackney on to Westminster Abbey where she descended and sought out the choir master who introduced her to Arthur Wellesley.

"Hello, Arthur, I'm Lady Elizabeth Rostov" Marion said shaking the small boy's hand "I'm a dear friend of your Mama. She sent me to collect you as she wants you to come home."

"Does she?" said the fair-haired boy unenthusiastically. "I usually only go home on Saturday afternoons. It's only Tuesday." He looked at the choirmaster with a face that pleaded with him not to let him go.

"Well, my dear, think of today as Saturday. Run along and get changed." Arthur looked at the choirmaster again.

"Off you go, Wellesley. Do as Lady Elizabeth says." The boy went to change out of his cassock. "I hope you can bring him back by this evening, madam, it is so important for him not to miss his Latin class."

Marion and Arthur were let out a door that opened on to Parliament Square. In front of them were the Houses of Parliament rising into the grey of a winter's day.

"Father works there" Arthur stated matter of factly. "Beastly job making decisions for the poor all the time."

Marion was taken aback by the young boy's snobbery. None of her children spoke like that, for if they did, she would have them whipped by Emily Brooks.

"You father is in Africa at moment is he not?" Marion inquired.

"I hope he has all the Boers shot." The boy said it with such venom Marion was momentarily shocked. "Mama says he's had one hundred and seventeen thousand put in concentration centres." His blue-eyes narrowed. "What do you think of the Boers?" He phrased the question in such a way that he sounded just like an old man.

"I don't think of wars at all" replied Marion caught off-guard. She was astounded by the boy's ability to accurately quote figures. Olive could barely count to a hundred as yet.

"Women never know anything" Arthur added emphatically. "Father says they want to have the vote, but I think they should keep clear of politics and leave it to us chaps."

Marion was partly amused, partly concerned that such a young boy had such fixed views.

"So are you going to be a politician like your father when you grow up?" She felt compelled to lead the conversation before he started asking her awkward questions about herself.

"Certainly not. They can be bought for as little as a thousand a year. I'm going to be a tycoon!"

"A tycoon? Well, that's a grand position to aim for." Marion was impressed by his certainty.

"It's quite easy. If I get into steel before the Big War, I'll make my fortune in two or three years."

"What Big War is this?" Marion asked.

"The Big War!" Arthur said again in an exasperated tone. "Everyone knows there has to be a big war every forty or fifty years."

"I didn't know that" said Marion "So how long have we got?" she asked with a smile. There was a child in him after all. She was getting to the real Arthur Wellesley, not the Arthur everyone else wanted him to be.

"Oh" thought Arthur "about ten, maybe fifteen years. It would be better if it was ten so I could make my fortune before I was twenty-one." Marion did not know whether to laugh or feel pity for the boy. "Can we walk home? I'm sick of going everywhere by carriage."

Marion decided it was best not to laugh at Arthur. He was an earnest soul who was nearer ninety than nine. They walked towards Belgravia via St. James's Park.

"What sort of tree is that?" he asked.

"That's a beech tree, Arthur."

"And that one?"

"That's an oak."

"So that's what an oak tree looks like" he uttered in great excitement. "We're always singing about oak trees." He ran across an expanse of grass toward the majestic English oak, and on reaching its base, threw his arms around it. "It's huge!" he called out to her.

At that moment, crossing the grass in a steady rustle of dress, Marion wanted to believe that Arthur was Patrick's son. Until then she had dismissed the possibility completely out of hand, but now seeing this little boy with his small arms around an oak tree with a girth endless times his size, she was seized by a maternal instinct to claim her as one of her own family.

Then suddenly, Arthur began to kick the tree. Marion took hold of him by the shoulders.

"What's the matter?"

"It's a beastly thing!" he declared bursting into tears. He began kicking Marion in the shins.

"Oww! What's got into you, you little wretch!"

"I'm not wretched! I'm not!" He broke free and hid behind the tree.

Marion took a quick look at her shins to see if there was any broken skin, before going round to the other side of the tree. The little boy was all-haunched up against the trunk and sobbing. She knelt down beside him and offered him a handkerchief.

"Here, wipe your eyes. Boy's shouldn't cry."

"Why not?" He took the handkerchief and blew his nose.

"Well, to tell you the truth, I don't honestly know. I think boys should cry more often." She gazed across the park to the Serpentine where a pair of old ladies were feeding the ducks. "Now tell me, what is the matter?" She put her arm around him and pulled him into her. He rested his head on her lap and lay there for a few moments until his sobbing ceased. It was a repeat of what had gone on the evening before with her husband. It seemed that the whole male world was in tears.

"Mama and Papa don't love me. Nobody loves me. Everyone things I'm horrid. The other boys bully me and say awful things about me. It's not fair."

Marion felt a pain in her heart. She had in her lap a little boy whose parents were privileged and wealthy. Yet, despite the advantages that such parentage gives a child, Arthur, by the way he spoke, sounded like a little orphan boy.

"Of course your mother loves you, and I'm sure your father is proud to have a son as intelligent and knowledgeable as you. Don't you worry about those other boys. Maybe they think no one loves them too? Perhaps they say awful things to you because you say awful things to them?" As soon as she said it, Marion knew the little boy would become indignant. He lifted his head.

"I don't! I want them to be my friends. Some of them go home in the evenings. Why can't I? I only live a mile and a half away." A sudden change can over him. "It's because Mama has boyfriends, that's why I can't go home. She doesn't want them to see me. She never thinks that maybe I don't want to see them either. I wish they would all go away with their horrid pipes and ugly beards and not wanting to kiss my Mama all the time. Papa calls me a little bastard. When he's home, he collects me from the Abbey, beats me, and makes me stay in my room without supper."

Marion felt sorry for the boy. He was bright, lively, and with the right guidance, he would achieve wonderful things. But as matters stood, his wish to be a tycoon would be just a wish, for Marion perceived that unless the boy was treated with more sensitivity and love, rather than put out of the way by his mother, and beaten by his father, he would have a disturbed childhood which would take a whole lifetime to reconcile.

It started to rain. The old women by the lake put up their umbrellas. Marion rose to her feet and put up her umbrella.

"Come now, Arthur. Let's get you home." She took his hand, and quite by surprise, he pressed the back of it against his cheek, then let go and threw his arms around her hips and abdomen and pressed her tightly. As a mother, she knew she had won his approval, and that he was thanking her for listening to him. She placed the flat of her hand on his head. " Come now, dear, I need to have a long talk with your mother."

He looked up at her and his look put beyond question any doubts she had. They hurried out of the park and took a carriage from the Palace to the Wellesley house in Grosvenor Place. Yes, there was no mistaking, Arthur had the eyes and good looks of Patrick, and Marion was damned if she was going to let them waste the life of her husband's son.

*

Maud Diver Wellesley was drunk on champagne in the middle of the afternoon. She was not alone. Her 'guest' was busy dressing himself.

"Shall we open another bottle, Joseph?" she asked the sixty-five year old man.

Joseph Chamberlain was the strongest, ablest, and most popular man in the Cabinet, but he was a coalitionist liberal unionist, and not a conservative, and thus had been denied the post of Prime Minister by Salisbury who allowed him the power of a co-premier, and on rare occasions more. He was a tall, clean-shaven, good-looking man with a full head of flaxen hair, and when fully dressed, he wore a monocle in his right eye. He was an immaculate dresser, and as Maud watched him dress, she noted how meticulously he fastened each button.

Despite his age, Chamberlain was a vigorous man, and he was always ready to please Maud if she wished it. She, by contrast, had become more interested in the old man's mind that far out-performed the agility of his body, for since his youth, he'd had a disdain for physical exercise and it showed.

"No thank you, my love. I have to report to the Cabinet later."

Maud put his glass of champagne down on the bedside table. "How are things in Africa? When will Diarmid be recalled?" As far as she was concerned, he hoped the Boer War would go on forever if Diarmid were a mediator. She did not want him home.

"Who can say? First Ladysmith, then Mafeking, it's never ending. Four hundred and fifty thousand men, and we still can't beat their fifty thousand. We haven't an ally and a friend in the world. The Americans have eased off a little, but the Germans have crossed to the other side for good. They've begun colonial expansion in a big way, and they mean business. In all, it's a terrible time. With the death of the Queen a great epoch has closed. Few credited her with much influence in state affairs, but I know better, the public underrated her grasp and capacity as much as they overrate Edward's. I'd rather have her any day to her son. It's grey days for England, unrest in the towns, the countryside going to waste, religious faith waning. I have this sense of an uncontrollable transition into the unknown, this feeling that the keys of power are bit by bit being transferred to new types of men, new nations. As a country, we've lost our grip on the world. Heaven save us if the Germans take their eyes off France and view us as their new number one enemy. Anyway, it is this war in Africa that makes me sleepless. I'm having the concentration camps transferred to my control. I've had reports from Diarmid that up to twenty thousand of the citizen population have died in Kitchener's camps already. The whole episode will come back to haunt me."

Joseph laced up his boots. Maud was partly infatuated by him, but he for his part was just lonely. The demands of state had left a vacuum in his personal life. Everyone he knew befriended him for political or financial advance. He knew that Maud had used him to get promotion for her husband, or rather, he suspected, used him to send her husband away. In such circumstances, he was not above accepting the reward of sexual favours.

Fully dressed, Maud escorted Joseph to the hallway while his carriage was brought around to the front of the house. They made their formal farewells, and Maud left him to be shown out by the manservant.

Outside, it was pouring with rain. The back wall of Buckingham Palace was being repointed for King Edward's coronation and the workers were sheltering under canvas awnings until the worst of the rain had passed. Not wishing to be recognised, he held his hat over his face and made a dash for his carriage. Just as he reached the carriage door, held open by Maud's man, he noticed a lady and a boy descending from a hackney. Recognising the lady, he quickly mounted the carriage step and inconspicuously watched from the interior as the woman and boy scurried through the open doorway of the Wellesley's house. The manservant gasped in horror, and fled after them.

The boy did not interest Joseph, but Marion Trainor did. He had always thought of her as one of the most beautiful women in London, and regretted that she had married a commercial traveller instead of himself after the death of his second wife. Maud Wellesley was not a patch on Marion Trainor, but he knew that life was for living and not wishing, and in a sombre mood, instructed his driver to take him to Downing Street.

*

"You have no right to burst into my house!

Get out at once!"

Maud took more sips of champagne. She was quite intoxicated.

"Mama, please ....." Arthur pleaded, trying to take the glass from her hand.

"Go away, you little brat." She raised her hand to strike him, but Marion intervened, and caught her by the wrist. Maud sobered slightly.

"Arthur, you're Mama is not feeling herself at the moment. Can you go to your room and change your clothes, my darling."

After an exchange of glances with Marion, Arthur did as he was told, and left the room. Marion closed the drawing room door behind him. She turned to face her adversary. When she had first laid eyes on Maud, she was shocked at how small she was. Marion had built up an image of Maud Wellesley in her mind and imagined her as a powerful, handsome woman who would be a force to reckon with. Instead, she found a rather small brunette with big eyes and lips that dominated her whole face. The rest of her was rather plain. She had that common English look that she saw so often, the weak chin, the curled in shoulders, the drooped bosom. In normal society she would pass for the daughter of a grocer or a milliner, there was nothing striking different about her that separated her from the ordinary run of the mill 'rose'. However, despite her drunken state, there was something sexual in her movements which reminded Marion of a cat, and she could tell, from the frightened look and barring of her teeth, that Maud Wellesley felt cornered in her own house.

"Now, Maud Wellesley, you will listen to my proposal, or you will be at the centre of a scandal which will bring the end for you, Wellesley, Joseph Chamberlain, and perhaps even the government itself."

"You don't frighten me. You're not the first irate wife I've had barging in here" she hissed holding on to the mantelpiece.

"I'm not here to frighten you, Missus Wellesley, I'm here to save you."

"Ha!" Maud laughed hysterically. "I've heard some good lies in my life, but that takes the cake."

"I am quite serious. I think you need help."

"Who the bleeding hell do you think you are? Do you think I need help from the wife of a failed husband? In all the years I've known him, he's been pathetic."

Marion remained calm. "I think you are the one who is pathetic. I have had a private detective watch this house from across the street for the last two weeks. He has made a fine list of the male visitors you have received in that time. Do you want to hear?"

"I never keep count. Maybe you could remind me" she said arrogantly. She had picked up that manner of reply from Diarmid. In this respect, they were their own worst enemies, their pride denying them the grace that sometimes saves the ignoble from defeat.

"He's listed the dates and times to the exact minute, night as well as day. I shall only read to you the number of occasions each of your callers came - The Colonial

Secretary, Joseph Chamberlain, four times, if you include just now. Count Hatzfeldt the German ambassador, thrice. The First Lord of the Treasury, Arthur J.Balfour, thrice. Lord President, Duke of Devonshire, twice. The son of the Colonial Secretary, Austen Chamberlain, twice. Secretary to the Treasury, Victor Cavendish, twice. Member of Parliament, Lloyd George, once. Edward, Prince of Wales, now King Edward, once. These of course are only the gentlemen that my man could visually identify. There were five other gentlemen of undisclosed identity, not including my husband, who visited you more than once. There were eight other gentlemen who visited you only once. In all that adds up to twenty-one if we exclude my husband. That averages out at one and a half a day."

Maud batted her eyelids, but it was obvious to Marion that she was embarrassed by the disclosure. She seemed lost for words. She knew she was in a tight position. She emptied her glass. "Do you intend to blackmail me then?"

"I am only concerned about one man - my husband. I want the twenty thousand pounds you blackmailed him out off."

"Don't be ridiculous, woman! I don't have that kind of money!"

Marion gazed at the sumptuous surroundings. "You are the one being ridiculous." She looked at the paintings on the wall and recognised a Gainsborough, a Landseer, a possible Goya, and an indisputable Rembrandt. "You'll have to sell something then, or I shall take such action that will show you up as the harlot that you are. In the meanwhile, you will terminate your liaisons with the men on this list and go to South Africa to be with your husband. Arthur will come to live with his father Patrick and I until such time that you can prove to me that you have reformed yourself. Then we may discuss sharing his upbringing together."

"You don't think I'm going to go along with your suggestions do you?" Maud was beside herself with anger. She was not concerned about losing her son; it was the thought of losing her position of influence with the most powerful men of the day.

"Yes, I sincerely believe you will. Arthur is leaving with me now, and if you try to stop me, I will go straight to the Daily News about your liaison with the German ambassador and the Colonial Secretary. That is evidence enough to have you indicted as a spy." She recalled Henry James's phrase. "Pillow talk I believe it is called. Your entire circle will be ruined, and you will go to prison."

Maud was devastated. She stood open mouthed propped-up by the mantle-piece. Prison? Slowly, her legs gave way, and Marion's greatest moment of triumph came as Maud sank into an armchair and gazed lifelessly up at the ceiling.

Marion, the battle won, opened the drawing room doors, crossed the hall and boldly marched upstairs and found the boy playing in a small damp bedroom with some toy soldiers. She picked him up, scooped the soldiers into her handbag, and carried the little boy down the stairs. She crossed the hall and stood at the entrance to the drawing room. Maud was still staring at the ceiling.

"Say goodbye to your Mama, Arthur."

"Goodbye, Mama" It was a prefunctionary declaration; there was no feeling in his farewell.

"You have one week, Mrs. Wellesley, to gather the money and have it deposited with my solicitor Mister Crum, or the matter will be out of my hands. Here is his card." She put it on a table.

With that, Marion turned with Arthur in her arms and strode purposefully past the servants. They would soon be out of a job, but that was not her concern. The manservant opened the front door, and once outside in the rain, Marion lowered Arthur into the waiting hackney, and then stepped into the carriage herself. Everything had gone according to plan, but she was still apprehensive that there would be a last minute confrontation with Maud about Arthur. She knew that she did not have the law on her side in this matter, and that if Maud proved awkward, she would not have the heart to deny a mother the custody of her own son. But Maud did not appear at the door, or look out the window. She had mentally abandoned her son many years before.

Marion instructed the driver to take them to Victoria Station.

"Am I not going back to the Abbey for my Latin lessons?" Arthur asked.

"No, you won't ever be going back there."

Marion, as a Roman catholic, did not approve of the Church of England. "You are coming home with me. I want you to meet someone very special."

"Is it Father Christmas?" he asked.

Marion gave him an enormous hug. "No, dear." She hesitated for a moment, inwardly giving thanks to God for giving them at last, a son of their own. "It is your real father."

4

As the youngest in the family, Olive was used to getting the most attention. The sudden appearance of a stranger in the midst of the family was at first novel, but sometime later unsettling. The shift of family focus to her new 'brother', pushed her more and more into the arms of Grandma Clarissa who unlike Arthur was not a rival for her parent's attention.

It was never quite explained to anyone in the family who Arthur was, though he did call Patrick 'Father' and Marion 'Auntie'. He joined Chloe and Olive in the schoolroom, though six months later, Chloe left for Roedean School for Girls to join her two sisters.

Brooky was amazed at Arthur's breadth of knowledge, but soon discovered that much of what he knew had been gleaned from listening to adult conversation. He was a very bright boy, but Olive was the better pupil as she was used to Brooky's methods of teaching and discipline. It was almost six months before Arthur went a week without getting a whipping. By then, it was time for Arthur to go off to public school. He was only one month older than Olive, but he was a boy. Olive had to wait another year before she could go to school. However, because of the introduction of electric trams by London Transport, and the increasingly efficient train service, Arthur was sent as a day-boy to Harrow.

Olive then, for the first time, was alone in the house during the day. Schooling took up less of the day as Brooky only had her to teach, so Patrick put up a swing for her in the branch of the garden oak. It hung by the side of a bank with a drop to the lower garden, and if she sat akimbo and pulled the ropes, she flew over the ground as if riding a horse. She had a whole garden to herself that was divided by lawns, banks, winding grass paths. Beyond the garden gate was open ground and fields with tall-uncut grass that Olive would crawl on hands and knees through for miles unseen. At the very far end of the fields were some cottages with very poor children, and from the grass, Olive watched them playing their games. She had heard about the slums, and the terrible living conditions there. They were not proper slums, not the awful places that Olive had seen in her travels with her mama in London, they were just one hundred and fifty year old Middlesex cottages that had gone into disrepair. However, the people living there were as poor as the dwellers in the London slums, and she was fascinated by what she saw. A number of the cottages were thatched and looked very picturesque and seemed to link town and country together in a piquant way. But from what Olive saw, the families living there had small provision for comfort or decency.

Behind the cottages ran the main railway line into the black busy hubbub of London, along which long trains puffed and rattled away on the sun gilt tracks until silence once more brooded over the cottages. On the other side of the track, greenly fat country stretched towards Fulwell and Strawberry Hill.

Then, one late-spring day, hiding in the grass, watching the cottage children play, Olive was discovered by a very thin little weedy boy with a pale brown face and languid brown eyes. He wore a peakless cap, and old red comforter, and a faded tattered smock. He looked as though he was very badly off. He had climbed the thorn-branch hedgerow on the far side of the field and circled back towards the cottages..

"Law bless!" he declared in surprise as he came upon her.

Olive, with the guilt of a spy let out a "Don't tell them I'm here, please."

"You a gal!" he let out. "We thought you a boy. It's a gal!" he shouted to the others taking her by the arm and marching her towards the cottages. The other children came swarming to meet them. Olive tried to struggle, but the thin boy was strong for his size, so she thought it best to pretend she did not want to run away.

In all, when they surrounded her there

were about eight or nine cottage children of various ages. It was the closest she had been to the children and the cottages, and she noticed how different each one was. They were all poorly dressed, brown faced, and thin, but each was one of a kind as they stated at her. They jostled her towards the cottages that like the children were each of a kind. One was two-storied, red brick walled, with a slated roof; another was of yellow-walled timber-panelled brick with a high low-hanging mossy thatch roof; another was white-washed brick and flint with cracked grey shutters that hung down like table-leaves. At some of the doors, women stood knitting.

"I can't say what she is" one of the children wheezed.

"I says she goo to school." another guessed.

"Just gone eleven" another said after eyeing her up.

From the looks on their faces and the way they spoke, the cottage children's wits were slower than Olive's. They spoke about her as though they acknowledged that she was their social superior, and the impact of it was painful to Olive. Although Olive's clothes may have been the sole point upon which their demeanour was based, Olive's straight-backed look of defiance in the face of the gang of grubby peasant children might also have had something to do with it.

"What's your name?" asked a little brown-faced fellow in a blue and white neckerchief, buskins, and a very ragged jacket.

Olive was not going to be ordered about. "Only if you tell me your names first" she said haughtily. This was something Brooky had drummed into her. If you know strangers names, they won't harm you for fear of being caught.

The cottage children looked at one another, and the thin boy, who was obviously their leader, gave a nod.

"I'm Jack. I'm gooin' thirteen." He then proceeded to introduce everyone else in his gang, from Den, the boy with the blue and white neckerchief who was eleven, down to Jack's little sister Dot, who was six. "Now, that's 'em. Whats' you called?"

"Olive Vivian Trainor" she pronounced boldly. There was a silence, then an enormous roar of laughter from the children. "What's so funny?" she said greatly concerned that they were laughing at her.

"Olive Vivian" imitated Den in a mock accent. He had removed his neckerchief and was dancing about in the mire of the lane with his neckerchief dangling from his fingertips. Suddenly he slipped in the mud and found himself bottom-down in an enormous cowpat. The rest of the children roared even louder than before, to the extent that even Olive burst out in a fit of hysterics.

The ice had been broken. By summertime, Olive had become firm friends with the cottage children, in particular with Jack and his sister Dot. Jack's father was an agricultural labourer. He had scant, steel grey hair, moistly wiped down on his weather beaten forehead, and white stubble on his chin. He wore corduroy trousers and a bone-button fustian jacket with a bare throat. Olive thought him the most interesting man she had ever seen, and felt quite in awe in his presence. She did not realise that he was trying to impress her.

"Yes, Miss, I can do any kind o' hagricult'ral labour. Ast anybody that knows me - I don't care who ye ast. I've worked for Mr Wilkes and Mr Farnham close by. I'll goo from the plough even to the builin' an' thetchin'. Law bless ye, Miss, I'm better off than some - moor so than many be here. But then you're days and days out o' work in the year. I reckon I don't get moor than eight months out o' the twelve; and my boy don't get that."

"Jack goes to school?" Olive said in a tone that meant she did not understand why Jack had to work.

"Yes, I goo to school" Jack confirmed. "To the chapel school. It begins nine a-Sundays. I don't goo to no school a-weekdays. I'm picking up dung for Mister Wilkes; I get him a cartload a week. Two barrelsful a day. Each of 'em takes about an hour to fill on the Richmond road. Miles, I s'pose, I walks. He gives me seven shillings a week. Rest o' my time I'm working in the fields, stone-picking, cow-keepin' an' likes. I should be glad to get summut else to do."

Olive had never for a moment thought that Jack had to work for a living. Up until then he had always appeared to be at leisure. He liked to fish, and a few days before, he'd taken her down to the Thames to fish for trout. She had to carry his bait pot which was full of earth-worms. At first she had been disgusted, but she got used to it. They caught nothing. On the way back Jack climbed a high tree to a crow's nest, and as Olive watched she thought him the most wonderful companion in the whole world. The nest had a full clutch of eggs. He needed both hands to get down the tree, so he put some of the eggs in his mouth, but they slipped out and smashed. They had been ready to hatch, for when the smashed, Olive saw the tiny red-skinned chicks dangling out of the broken shells.

On another occasion she went with him on a cart to collect hay and came back on top of it. The sense of danger made it exciting as the cart jogged along the tracks. Jack told her about the time that one of the cottage boys had hid in a haycock and one of the labourer's, not knowing he was there, had put a pitchfork through the boy's eye, and that he was blind in that eye to that day. Thereafter, Olive always watched out for the one-eyed cottage boy, but she never saw him.

She introduced Arthur to Jack, but he did not take to him, nor he to Jack, but Arthur found a friend in Dot, and took her hand through the fields and along the lanes, telling her stories about a little boy called Philibert and Know-a-bit the Fairy who answered Philibert's questions on all sorts of things like what skin was, or what the moon was made of. After awhile, Dot called Arthur Know-a-bit, while the rest of the cottage children called Arthur Know-it-all.

However, Olive's friendship with Jack and the others came an abrupt end when it was discovered that Arthur had contracted smallpox and that a number of the cottage children, including Dot, had caught it too. The cottages were fumigated and everyone vaccinated.

*

When Maud Wellesley was told that her son had died in the smallpox epidemic that was sweeping London, it was Diarmid Wellesley who came to the Trainor household to challenge Patrick to a duel.

The Trainor household was in double mourning, for Pope Leo XIII had also died, and it came as an utter shock when Wellesley arrived unannounced. He barged his way into the house passed the servants, knocked over a frail Clarissa who challenged him, and came upon Marion kneeling before an effigy of Christ in the drawing room. Without a moment's hesitation he strode across the room, picked up the effigy, and threw it into the fire.

"That's what I think of your religion, you swines!" Marion had no idea who the madman in her house was. "You've killed my son!" Wellesley ran his cane along the mantelpiece and knocked a lifetime's collection of mementos on to the marble hearth where they smashed. "Where is the bastard!" He picked up a chair and threw it against the glass of the book-cabinet that ran the length of one of the walls. "Where is that coward Trainor!" He grabbed Marion by the throat, and then hit her across the face with the back of his hand. He sent her flying, and her head cracked against the side of the harmonium, and she lay there concussed.

Olive had heard the commotion and descended the stairs in leaps and bounds just in time to catch Wellesley thrashing her mother with his cane as she lay on the floor.

"Mama! Mama!" She ran to Wellesley and grabbed his arm, as he was about to bring his cane down on her mother's head. Wellesley grabbed Olive by her hair and dragged her across the room to the fireplace, and had the servants not burst in and lain their hands on him, he would have pushed her face into the fire.

With a roar, Wellesley threw them all off, and with a final fury of blows brought down on the backs of the servants, he burst out of the drawing room and went rampaging through the house searching for Patrick. He encountered Emily Brooks in the schoolroom and lashed out at her so violently, there was a loud crack as he broke her arm.

There was not a man in the house. Patrick was out on business, and there were no other men in the Trainor household. It was filled with the shrieks and screaming of woman reduced to hysteria by the mad actions of Wellesley.

"I'll be back for the Irish bastard!" he roared as he left the weeping household as quickly as he had entered. He fled out into the street and into a waiting automobile, and was gone.

The mayhem Diarmid Wellesley caused in the Trainor household was incalculable. Marion had a fractured skull, two broken ribs, and bruising to her face and body that took three weeks to subside. Clarissa lost the use of her legs and was confined to a wheelchair for the rest of her days. Miss Brooks, with her broken arm, was so traumatised, she had to resign her position as the Trainor governess. Mrs. Bradford the housekeeper pretended that she had not been hurt, but in fact she sustained a back injury that required constant nursing. Daisy the housemaid was treated for shock, and Olive, her scalp being sore from having her hair yanked out, was sent off to Ireland to recuperate with her Granma and Granpa Trainor in Killarney. The other girls were kept on at school for the half-term vacation until the whole matter was sorted out.

Patrick Trainor was furious and ready to murder Diarmid Wellesley, but Marion refused blankly to let him take any action. The matter was out of their hands and in those of the police. This time, she reassured him that Wellesley had destroyed himself.

Wellesley was charged with assault and grievous bodily harm, but on account of his position in the government, he was not arrested. The police were in awe of him. He had only recently returned to England in triumph, having seen the conclusion of the war with the Boers, being present at the surrender in Vereeniging. Maud, who had joined him in South Africa, had told him nothing of Marion's ultimatum, or of the fact that Arthur had been taken out of the Abbey school, and gone to live with the Trainors.

Diarmid was on top of the world and expecting promotion into Cabinet, for his uncle Salisbury was stepping down as Prime Minister, and Arthur Balfour, his second cousin, was taking over and reshuffling the Cabinet. He had been promised the post of Chief Secretary for Ireland, taking over from George Balfour, Arthur's brother, and he was looking forward to knocking the Irish nationalists on the head.

He went to the Abbey to see his son, but soon discovered that he was not there. Maud, still trying to cover her infidelities, said that she had sent him for private schooling, and Diarmid, taken up by the affairs of the state, believed her. Then came the news of his death by smallpox, and in a drunken stupor, Maud told Diarmid of Marion Trainor's blackmail of her over Joseph Chamberlain. She knew that Diarmid would forgive her for having an affair with Chamberlain as it had furthered his career, but she also knew that he would beat her senseless if he learned of the others. She also failed to admit telling him that he was not the father of Arthur.

Diarmid could not understand why the Trainor's had taken Arthur other than to hurt him. He convinced himself that they had deliberately let him die of smallpox, and that it was part of Patrick Trainor's revenge for the way Diarmid had treated him at school. As for Marion Trainor, he thought her a scheming bitch for blackmailing twenty thousand pounds out of his wife. One wrong deserved another. If he went and maimed her for what she had done, he felt confident that she would not report it to the police in case the story of blackmail emerged. With this in mind, he had gone and soundly beaten the vixen and her household, never for a moment dreaming that his wife had not told him the whole story. It was therefore with some surprise he found himself charged on five accounts of assault, though he was convinced that the charges would be dropped if Marion Trainor was reminded that she was a blackmailer. He sent her a letter demanding twenty thousand pounds to be repaid to him, or he would inform the police that she had blackmailed his wife, stolen his son, and deliberately killed him by exposing him to smallpox.

Diarmid began to worry when the date of the trial loomed nearer and the Trainors had not replied to his letter. He knew that if found guilty, he would not only lose any chance of a Cabinet post, but that he might also have to step-down from the Commons, and put his seat up for re-election. His political career would be finished. It was time to settle the score with Patrick Trainor. The beating of his wife had not flushed him out. What sort of man was that?

Diarmid sent his man Roberts to challenge him to a duel. The conditions of the contest were that if Patrick lost, all charges against Diarmid were to be dropped, and the

Trainor's were to pay twenty thousand, plus another twenty thousand pounds for the loss of Arthur. If Patrick won, Diarmid would announce publicly that the loss of his son had deranged him, that he was sorry, and that he would compensate the injured.

Marion knew that Wellesley was offering them nothing that they had not already won, but she could not get Patrick to see this. He was intent in facing Wellesley in a private duel in the woods of Buckinghamshire using handguns. It was as if time had stopped still and that the twentieth century had not arrived. Duelling was a thing of the past that had been outlawed after the Napoleonic wars, and Patrick knew nothing about guns. Diarmid, on the other hand, had been a hunting and shooting man in India and Africa, as well as England and Ireland.

The meeting took place in the afternoon before the trial in a clearing in a private estate near Princes Risborough. Each had been allocated the latest Browning automatic pistol with one round in the breech. Wellesley had arrived in his steering wheel driven 40hp Mors, and was waiting for Trainor to show in his clumsy tiller-held Delahaye. It was cloudy day, but warm, and Wellesley, dressed in shirt sleeves and waistcoat stood chatting to his second Roberts, an army man, smoking a cigarette and talking about the war.

"Damn the man! Where is he?"

Time went by and Patrick did not show. In fact, Marion had convinced Patrick that nineteenth century customs could not solve twentieth century problems. On the morning of the duel, having made love to him for what she thought might be the last time, he had acquiesced, and seen the light.

"I'm not going to give that bully-boy the pleasure of blowing my brains out. I'm going to have my breakfast, and instead of going duelling, I'm going to take you shopping and buy you whatever you want." Marion was overjoyed at his decision. She pulled him to her and manipulated his manhood. "Wellesley's going to jail, and that's that" he said as she eased herself on to him. "I'll make sure he goes down." He gave way to her smooth hip movements. "My God, he will ...." She placed her lips on his and silenced him.

So they went shopping, and Marion bought some of the new corsets designed for active women that were all the rage.

They were still in London, when there was a terrible banging on their front door in Teddington. The servants, still wary of any visitors, saw who it was and informed the housekeeper.

"It's him, Mrs. Bradford!" Daisy declared.

"You would think we were being besieged like Mafeking" she hinted without fear. The rest of the staff were terrified, so much so, they ran and hid themselves in the cellar.

"Open up you damned coward!" Wellesley had been drinking on the drive back from Buckinghamshire. He was livid. Suddenly there was an almighty roar. Mrs. Bradford had thrown a bucket of dirty water over him from an upstairs window.

"That'll dampen your spirits, you madman! Now clear orff before the police arrive."

"I'll be back, you old hag! You killed my son!" Wellesley was soaked to the skin, but his anger was still burning strong.

"If I was you, cock, I'd ask me wife whose son it was, for it wasn't yours, you cuckold!"

"What did you say?" Wellesley roared.

Mrs. Bradford slammed shut the window and made rude gestures at him from behind the glass.

"Come on, Wellesley, old chap, you've had your chance." Roberts was embarrassed. Many of the neighbours servants in the street were looking out from behind their curtains.

"What did she say, Robbo?"

"Nothing, Wellesley. Let's take you home. Trainor's not here. Let's not get into trouble with the law. We've got some unlicensed firearms in the car."

"He was always a squealing coward. Can't keep his Paddy mouth shut!! That's what's wrong with Trainor, he's a faggot like his old man. He's never been a gentleman. Not like us, Robbo, eh?"

Roberts bundled him into the Mors, threw a blanket over him, and drove him home. By the time they got to Grosvenor Place, Wellesley had sobered a little. He told Roberts to take the car for the night and pick him up in the morning for his court appearance. Roberts wanted to see him to bed in case he did anything foolish, but Wellesley would not hear of it. He took the blanket from the car and sent Roberts on his way. Roberts had failed to notice that he had also picked up the two Browning pistols.

Once inside the house, the words of the Trainor's housekeeper were ringing in his ears. Cuckold? He knew his wife had been repeatedly unfaithful to him, but Arthur had been his offspring, Maud was not that careless. Or was she? He placed the guns on the hallway table.

"Maud! Maud!" he began shouting.

Maud was running a bath. In Africa she had managed to straighten herself out by cutting down on alcohol. She no longer needed a drink in the afternoon, but that did not mean she had gone completely dry. She still liked a good drink in the evening.

Maud could not hear Wellesley because of the running water. He went upstairs. In normal circumstances the servants would have told him where their mistress was, but when he was in a foul mood, they avoided him as best they could. By chance he came upon Nancy, Maud's personal maid.

"Where is the slut!!"

Nancy knew what was about to happen; she had seen the master of the house at his most violent before. First he would take it out on the furniture, then anybody who got in his way. She pitied Maud Wellesley, for he was an utter brute who battered his wife whenever it suited him. It amazed Nancy that he had never broken Mrs. Wellesley's spirit. Any lesser woman would have given up her adulterous ways, but Mrs. Wellesley appeared to relish the beatings as proof of her husband's love for her. It was a marriage made in hell.

Nancy pointed to the bathroom, for she knew if she told him anything but the truth, she would get a backhander from him. Diarmid careered into the bathroom.

Maud was sitting naked on the side of the bath when Diarmid burst in. At first she thought it was Nancy, but in an instant she saw Diarmid looming towards her with his arm raised. He knocked her into the bath with a blow on the bridge of her nose. As she spluttered and thrashed in the bath, he pushed her head under the water and held it there until nearly all of the life was out of her, then dragged her out of the bath and bathroom by the hair. As she struggled and clawed at the carpet, he jerked her along the upper hall rug to the head of the stairs. For good measure he gave her some kicks in the abdomen, and as she gasped for breath, he pulled her head-first down the long flight of stairs to the reception hall below. Still holding her by her hair, he picked up one of the Browning pistols from the hall-table and put the end of the barrel to her mouth and pushed it to the back of her throat.

Maud, her naked body covered in carpet burns, kick marks, cuts and bruises sustained from the abuse she had just undergone, choked for breath. Her eyes were already half closed from the swelling caused by her broken nose, and she had no feeling in her right leg below the knee. She was terrified beyond anything she had ever experienced before; she knew Diarmid had finally gone insane. She could put up with being knocked about the bedroom or strangled, but this time he had gone too far. He had always tried to dominate her and never succeeded. Now, he looked capable of murder.

"Why didn't you tell me, you whore!! You never told me that Arthur wasn't my son! " He knocked her head against the wall, and Maud felt as though the pistol had gone through the back of her throat. She gurgled and blood began to seep from her mouth. He had knocked out her front teeth. "Of all the men it was Trainor's child. Wasn't it???" He lowered himself on to her and sat astride her and took the gun barrel out of her mouth. "Speak up you filthy cow!"

Maud was past caring. She saw her front teeth lying on the carpet and her right leg bent at an angle that confirmed that it was smashed. She could see the bone sticking out of the side of her leg. She was in so much pain she could not talk. Diarmid cocked the trigger on the gun.

"Yes ...." she croaked "Pat Trainor. I've always been in love with Pat." Even to the end she could lie.

For Diarmid it was the end. His own wife had betrayed him and he could not forgive her. He squeezed the trigger and the recoil almost broke his wrist as Maud's brains splattered up the hall wall and across Diarmid's face and shirt. He put the gun to his own head and pulled the trigger again, but it clicked empty. Then he remembered there was only one round in the gun. He stretched out his fingers and fumbled for the other Browning, picked it up, put it to his forehead and pulled the trigger. The bullet went clear through his head and lodged in the staircase.

There was stillness and a silence the house had never known before. Nancy descended the stairs on tip-toe, but when she saw the two blood drenched bodies slumped together against the hallway wall, she burst, in a fit of screaming, out of the house and along passed the polished doors of Grosvenor Place towards Hyde Park Corner, so that within an hour, all of London knew what had taken place.

5

Olive had reached the perfect age. It was that age in life when a child does not want to be young yet does not want to get any older. Some children never have this feeling, but most, at one stage of their development or another, feel the approach of adulthood and want to remain, like Peter Pan, a child forever.

Olive's perfect age came upon her while she was staying with her grandparents in Killarney. She was ten, and she had no desire to think about being eleven. She lived every day for the moment, and went to bed every night impatient for the next day to start. By wishing each day to start, she was likewise aware that each day brought her nearer to her eleventh birthday. There was no time to waste; she would rise with the larks; dress in a hurry; rush her breakfast; and flee like a fairy out of the old castle and take to the hills where she was free of the worries of growing up.

Patrick and Vivian Trainor could not keep up with their energetic granddaughter. She was no a free spirit they could neither stable or harness. Her energy had them in a whirl, and the most they could do was to make sure she ate four meals a day and had a constant supply of clean clothes. The rest of the time, Olive amused herself by wandering over the hills, exploring the glens and woods of the Killarney district, wading the streams or swimming in the loughs, never tired, never sad, constantly curious about everything that the world presented to her.

After the confines and the brutality of London life, the openness of Ireland had liberated her spirit. She blocked out the tragic death of Arthur and the horror of Diarmid Wellesley's assault on her mother, and like some wild horse, filled her head with the wind and rain and the smell of turf, which she loved so dearly, in preference to the coal-smoke of dull, decaying London. Ireland was alive! The deer, the hares, the grouse, the squirrels, the foxes, and of course, the horses - these were her friends. In her child's mind these could not be taken away from her.

Then, one day, she came upon a shooting party slaughtering scores of grouse, and later, on Torc Estate, a pack of hunt dogs tearing a fox to pieces. The slaughtering of the grouse she came to terms with, but not the fox, the scream of the animal over the baying of the dogs sent her flaying into the animals with a large stick. But the dogs had tasted blood and would not let go of their quarry.

"In the name of God, girl! Leave off my dogs!"

Olive turned to see an elderly man mounted on a fine bay. He was dressed in a hunting outfit. Two younger men came galloping up behind him.

"Call them off, Rigby" the old man ordered one of the younger riders. Rigby called the dogs off, then dismounted and went to the fox and held it up.

"It's the old vixen. Looks as though we've tracked the wrong fox, Mr. Riley."

"We've uncovered a young one, though" he said looking at Olive. "Do you know you are on private land, girl?" He had a smile with an evil twist to it. "What's your name, lass?" His tone had softened, almost as if he realised that he was being too harsh to the pretty young thing with the dark looks whose skirt was splattered with the fox's blood.

Olive did not know whether to give her name or not, but she remembered her training. "I will only tell you my name if you tell me who you are."

"A proper educated little madam." The old man and his companions laughed. "Very well. I am the Honourable Judge John Riley. This gentleman is the Honourable George Douglas, QC. And that is Shaun Rigby, our gamekeeper." Riley leant back in his saddle. "Now, my lass, your name, please."

Olive was not intimidated. She had not spent her whole life in London in isolation. Her mother and father knew lots of legal men, and of course, her grandfather was a lawyer. They were all stuffy old men as far as Olive were concerned.

"I am Olive Vivian Trainor" she declared.

Riley's face turned red. The name of Trainor was still a thorn in his side, even after the elapse of thirty years since the dissolve of their legal partnership.

"Are you related to the Trainors of Castlelough?" asked Douglas.

"That I am" she returned boldly "The finest family in all of Ireland." She had often heard her father say that to guests who had inquired about the family in Ireland.

Riley let out a cynical laugh, while Douglas winced. The gamekeeper kept his head down.

"Rigby" Riley ordered "escort the girl to the police station in Killarney. I want her charged with poaching." There was an evil look in his eye. "Rigby ..." he said again.

The gamekeeper seemed reluctant to do as he was told, but he knew his job was worth more than his sense of right and wrong.

"Cmon, then Georgie, let's get back to the house" Riley said to his companion. "We'll take the dogs with us. Rigby, you bring the fox up to the big house later."

"Aye, aye, sir." Rigby was a giant of a man, and he seemed ill at ease taking orders.

"Let's go then, me lass."

Olive did not know what was going to happen, but she knew she had done nothing wrong, and followed after Rigby in the direction of Killarney. They got talking, and Rigby found out whom she was.

"Yer grandfather was a souper" he told her.

"What is that?" she asked.

"A man who changes his religion for money."

"My grandfather did that?"

"Aye, lass, but he chang'd back again once he'd spent the money. I've a lot of respect for your ol' grand-father, he's done a lot for the common Irish man."

"Do you not you like the Judge, then?" she probed.

"Jesus, if a man's expected to lick his employer's arse, then he'd be a fool if he liked it. Every last soul in Kerry hates Judge Riley. He's a Brit, and who wants to t'ank him for transporting and hanging t'eir dear ones."

Shaun Rigby led Olive through the trees of Torc Estate until they could see the tower of Muckross Abbey. He stopped her by a stonewall.

"This is the estate boundary. Now, if I so happen to look t'other way, well, would it be me fault if ye were to leap over the wall and be gone like the wind." Olive did not understand what he meant. She had never run away from anything before. He turned is back on her, but she did not move. Rigby looked sideways over his shoulder. "Jesus, are ye an eggit or some'it. Is yer brain in yer bum. And I t'ought you Trainor's smart an' all." He turned away again.

This time Olive understood everything. She scrambled over the wall and ran pell-mell for the grounds of the abbey. She looked back and saw Shaun Rigby still standing facing the other way. Next time she looked, he was gone.

*

In each new century since the beginning of time, wonderful things have been discovered. In the nineteenth century, more amazing things were found than any century before. In our own century, thousands of things still more astounding have been brought to light. At first people refuse to believe that a strange new thing has occurred, then they begin to hope it cannot be done, then they see it can be done - then it is done and all the world wonders why it was not done centuries before.

The foxhunt incident made Olive realise that Ireland was not free. It had never entered her head that Irish people did not want to be part of Britain. Like a powerful electric battery illuminating a lamp, her thought's had suddenly been switched on. She knew that sad or bad thoughts getting into her mind were as dangerous as letting smallpox fever enter her body. She knew if she let such thoughts stay there after they had got in she might never get over them as long as she lived. But try as she might, she could not empty her head of the fact that she had become aware of Ireland's differences.

Her grandmother Vivian was not happy that her only grandchildren were being brought up to think of themselves as English. She had hoped that perhaps one of them would return to the old country when they grew up, and it was on Olive she now pinned these hopes. At the age of sixty-three,

Vivian was as ardent in her work to bring about Irish independence as she had been in her youth, but the movement was in a slum. She, by way of her husband, had helped to push for the rights of peasant tenants to purchase the land they farmed, and at long last, Wyndam, the Irish Secretary, was pushing through the Land Purchase Act. It came as a relief to the nationalists to hear of the death of Diarmid Wellesley, for had he replaced Wyndam in the post, the Act would have been quashed. News of Wellesley's death astounded Olive, but it gave her such a feeling of joy and elation, Vivian thought her glee over-ecstatic, and reprimanded her for finding happiness in other people's misfortune. Secretly however, Vivian was also overjoyed, for Diarmid Wellesley had given their family no end of trouble, and she had always believed that he would come to a sticky end. Patrick Snr. was more circumspect, for he felt that the appointment of Wellesley as Irish secretary might have been the very thing to have tipped the scales for the nationalists, for Wyndam, as a popular secretary, pleased the Irish people too much for them take up arms against him.

Olive was totally unaware of these goings on. However, after the incident in Torc Estate, she felt more confined, hemmed-in, for the wide open spaces she had taken such easy access of, appeared now as parcels of land owned by Lord Somebody or Sir Someone, and that spoiled everything. She began spending more time with her grandmother who taught her a few words of Gaelic and pointed out the hiding places of the little people. They rowed out to Innisfallen Abbey that Vivian had helped to restore, and one fine morning, she drove her automobile to where her beloved Volcano had crashed over Torc Falls. From there, they climbed Mangerton Mountain together to visit the Devil's Punch Bowl.

"The last time I was here was the year before your father was born." Vivian thought back to the crazy days of her youth. She told Olive of the legend as they huffed and puffed their way to the top. "Now, me girl, I'll not be having you drinking the water, you're far too young."

Nevertheless, when they reached the placid black lake, they were both so thirsty, they took long soaks of water, before bathing their feet in the icy lake.

"Well, then" Vivian said half-jokingly "I hope we don't both have babies now."

"Look" pointed Olive.

"What are you pointing at?" Her grandmother's eyes were not as good as they once were.

"It is a man. Look, he's drinking the water."

"Do you think he'll have a baby?" Vivian said tongue-in-cheek.

"No, do not be silly, granma" Olive replied. "I know men do not have babies ....." The man had caught sight of them, and began walking their way at a vigourous pace. "Look who it is! It is Shaun Rigby."

Vivian knew the name well. He was one of the Brotherhood. What was he doing at the top of Mangerton Mountain? When he came closer, she recognised him for herself.

"Top of the morning to you, Mrs. Trainor, and to you Miss Olive." He seemed flustered.

"What's wrong, Shaun?" Vivian queried.

Shaun Rigby glanced at Olive, and asked Vivian with his eyes if it was safe to talk in front of her. Vivian nodded.

"There was trouble at Kenmare last night. The Constabulary was waiting for us. They shot Hughes, O'Hare, and wounded Morrison. They'd have had me on the Killarney road if I hadn't legged it over the mountain.

"Did they get a look at ye?"

"Not at all. It was as black as Africa last night, that's why we didn't see them hiding by the boat shed. They opened fire before we even got the guns on the beach." The mention of guns made Olive's ears prick. She looked at her grandmother who seemed to take the news with some agitation. "Some souper tipped them off, so help me God."

"Morrison'll talk. They'll be waiting for you at Torc." Vivian clenched her teeth. She took her feet out of the water and dried them with the hem of her scarf. "Here's what you'll do. Take Olive with you down to Castlelough." Olive's eyes opened wide. "You'll go to the stable and saddle yoursel' a horse and a pony while she goes into the house and fetches you some clothes and money." She described where the money and clothes could be found. "Then she'll travel with you as your daughter as far as Tralee where you'll leave her with my brother O'Hara. Declan will guide you from there and pass you onto the Brotherhood in Galway where you can hide 'til things die down. If you're stopped by the Constabulary you'll give your name as James Riley, the son-in-law of the Judge."

"Jesus, he's never had a child" Shaun interrupted, not happy with the alias.

"They'll never know that. And mercy, what Irishman can honestly say he's never been a father?"

So the plan was hatched.

"Will ye be alright leaving ye here to find yer own way down?" asked Shaun.

"Why it's a grand day is it not, Shaun Rigby. I'll be as right as rain."

Olive gave her grandma a kiss and set off quickly down the mountain with the gamekeeper. He took her hand much of the way, and when she tired, he carried her on his back until they reached the Torc Cascade where Vivian had left the motorcar. An hour later, by a secluded and a little known route, they came to Castlelough Tower, the home of the Trainors.

Castlelough was an old peel tower that had functioned as a small castle in times of trouble. It was said that it stood on the site of an ancient Celtic stronghold that was burnt by the Normans, but no one knew for sure, only the tower remained. When the Trainor's bought it in '72, it had changed hands five times in the previous eight years. It was there that Olive's father had spent his childhood, and when she had first seen it, she compared it with their home in

Teddington, and automatically thought that her father had come down in the world. Later, she changed her mind, for she realised the Tower was cold and damp, and that apart from the lower rooms, reception area and kitchens, it was a poor place to live. The Trainors should have been wealthy enough to restore the entire building to habitation, for Patrick Trainor Snr was a very successful barrister who frequently took cases to the High Court in Dublin. Then, after hearing how much money had been spent restoring part of Innisfallen Abbey, and now, the connection with the Brotherhood which made grandma Vivian give money freely to help the cause of independence, Olive realised where the Trainor wealth was going. They were putting up with a cold, damp castle tower, in order to save the culture, and promote the cause of Ireland.

While Shaun saddled a horse for himself and a pony for Olive, she went to her grandfather's closet and took out some gentleman's clothes for him, then went to the study and counted out ten pounds from a money box she found behind some false books. She re-emerged from the Tower to find Shaun waiting with the horse and pony. He took the clothes and went into one of the stalls to change. Just then, O'Donahue, the old servant who was now almost ninety, appeared in the courtyard with a wheel barrel of logs.

"G'day, Miss. Yer' going riding with the master, Miss" he said putting the wheelbarrow down. "It's a fine horse he has, not an ounce tha's not pure t'ough'r-bred." Shaun Rigby appeared from the stall. The old man saw him as plain as day, dressed in his master's clothes, but chose to mind his own business. He had been in Ireland all his life, and he knew that there was always strange goings on that were best left unexplained. He picked the wheelbarrow up again. "Hav' a nice ride now with the master, Miss." He shuffled away across the courtyard, pushing the wheelbarrow, which squeaked with each turn of the wheel. As he reached the end of the courtyard he put the wheelbarrow down again, turned, and with the rub of a finger on his old crooked nose, croaked "Aye, mind now, ye don't break the legs o' the animals at the roadblock on Deenagh Bridge." He picked up the wheelbarrow again and turned the corner.

Heeding the old man's warning, they circumvented the town by way of Cock Hill, and from above Prospect House, watched the traffic coming out of Killarney along the Tralee road being stopped by the Constabulary. They turned up and climbed across the hills and over by Scartaglen, and crossed the Tralee road near Castleisland just as night was falling. Shaun decided to risk travelling the last eleven miles along the road. He did not want to risk Olive being thrown in the dark into a brackish bog hole which she would not come out of again.

They travelled without incident, and arrived, after some wrong turnings, at the house of Declan O'Hara, Olive's great uncle.

Olive was put to bed, and in the morning when she woke saddle sore and stiff, Shaun Rigby had gone, passed on by the Brotherhood to a safe haven in Galway. Later that day, Olive was collected by her grandma in her automobile and taken back to Killarney. Great-uncle Declan arranged for a man to ride the horse and pony back.

After such an adventure, the rest of Olive's stay in Kerry was spent listening for news about Shaun Rigby, but she heard none. If there was any, she was told nothing. She detected an air of secrecy, mostly from her grandpa Trainor. He had been away during the whole incident, and it was strange that he returned the day after it all happened, and no one mentioned a word of it to him. Olive tried to talk to him about it on several occasions, but each time he told her that he was very busy with important cases that needed his immediate attention, and sent her away. Yet, when he felt like it, he would play with and take her into the shops in the town and spoil her with sweets and girl things that only grandfather's know how to do.

"Granpa ...." Olive asked him when they were taking soda in an ice-cream parlour "what was my father like when he was my age?"

"Oh" thought Patrick Snr. He tried to recall his son at that age, but there were very few things that had stuck in his mind. "When he was born he was an ugly little child, everyone said so, though not to our faces. He wasn't pleased or interested in anything, and he was a very sickly, bore, and wretched child. Then we began to push him about for his own good, for he was a hysterical, half-crazy little hypochondriac who knew nothing of sunshine or the wild outdoors. Then his mind gradually filled itself with robins and blackbirds, bog land cottages crowded with children, crabbed old gardeners like O'Donahue, and common Connemara housemaids like Colly, who pushed him to stand on his own two feet. Life began to come to him, his blood ran healthily through his veins, and strength poured into him like a flood. It was a surprising transformation, and just in time to get him into boarding school. We didn't see much of him after that except at vacation time."

"Did you not miss him?" she asked

"Oh, I missed him terribly. If I had to bring Patrick up again, I would have kept him at home until he was much older. But, when he was young, there were not many schools in Kerry, and sending him away seemed the right thing to do. See, Olive, parents have to live the rest of their lives with the knowledge that they could have done better than they did for their children. A parent can never give a child everything the child needs, there is always something lacking, something that is missed at the right time or done at the wrong moment that they regret later. In Patrick's case it was my failure to teach him all the things that a father is meant to teach a son. I was always away on legal business, and in his early years he was left too much with your grandma and Colly. I failed as a man as I didn't enjoy fishing or sport, and I left it to O'Donahue to teach him those things. But O'Donahue was already an old man in those days, and he was more like a grandfather to him than a second father. Then came the boarding school, and everything was fine until all the fuss with Wellesley and his gang. Maybe your father will tell you about that someday."

That's what Olive hated most about grown-ups, they never finished a story, they only told part of it, and as children they were always promised that they would hear the rest when the grew up. Olive could not imagine what had happened to her father at boarding school, but now that she was approaching her eleventh birthday, she would be joining her sisters.

"I cannot wait to go to boarding school."

"Children can't wait for anything can they?"

It was a question that she was not expected to answer. "So, would you like another soda."

"Yes, please!" she shouted gleefully in her prime English accent that made everyone turn around and stare at her.

Patrick shook his head and smiled. For most of his adult life he had been fighting against English control of Ireland, only to discover that he had perpetuated the entire system, by producing English grandchildren.

Olive did not know what she was. At that moment in life, she was at the peak of innocence, at the dawn of worldly knowledge. As yet, she had made no judgements about herself, for it was the most wonderful time of her life. She was, as we have already been told, the perfect age.

ROBBIE MOFFAT

The author was born and schooled in Glasgow. He took a degree in English language and Literature at Newcastle University. He began writing when he was seventeen and has a had a career as a poet, novelist, playwright and screenwriter. He is best known for his feature film work in which he is also a director and producer.
His prose writing as been overshadowed by this. He wrote his first novel when he was twenty two and continued to write novels for the next twenty years. None of them were published.
The rediscovery of his prose work has lead to a recent spate of publications that has lead to a resurgence of interest in his prose work.